Dream of You

Also From Jennifer L. Armentrout

Forever With You
Fall With Me

By J. Lynn
Stay With Me
Be With Me
Wait For You

The Covenant Series
Daimon
Half-Blood
Pure
Deity
Elixer
Apollyon

The Lux Series
Shadows
Obsidian
Onyx
Opal
Origin
Opposition

The Dark Elements
Bitter Sweet Love
White Hot Kiss
Stone Cold Touch
Every Last Breath

A Titan Novel
The Return

Standalone Novels
Obsession
Frigid
Scorched
Cursed
Don't Look Back

Gamble Brothers Series
Tempting The Best Man
Tempting The Player
Tempting The Bodyguard

Dream of You

A Wait For You Novella

By Jennifer L. Armentrout

1001 Dark Nights

EVIL EYE
CONCEPTS

Dream Of You
A Wait For You Novella
By Jennifer L. Armentrout

1001 Dark Nights
Copyright 2015 Jennifer L. Armentrout
ISBN: 978-1-940887-39-5

Foreword: Copyright 2014 M. J. Rose
Published by Evil Eye Concepts, Incorporated

Acknowledgments from Jennifer L. Armentrout

I can't start off these acknowledgements without thanking my agent Kevan Lyon, who has always tirelessly worked on my behalf. A huge thank you to Liz Berry, the 1001 Dark Nights team, and everyone who worked on Dream of You. Thank you to my other publicist with the most-est K.P. Simmons for helping do everything to get the word out about the book.

I would go crazy if it weren't for these following people: Laura Kaye, Chelsea M Cameron, Jay Crownover, Sophie Jordan, Sarah Maas, Cora Carmack, Tiffany King, and too many more amazing authors who are an inspiration to list. Vilma Gonzalez, you're an amazing, special person, and I love you. Valerie Fink, you've always been with me from the beginning, along with Vi Nguyen, (Look, I spelled your name right), and Jessica Baker, among many, many other awesome bloggers who often support all books without the recognition deserved. THANK YOU. Jen Fisher, I heart you and not just for your cupcakes. Stacey Morgan—you're more than an assistant, you're like a sister. I'm probably forgetting people. I'm always forgetting people.

A special thank you to all the readers and reviewers. None of this would be possible without you and there isn't a thank you big enough in the world.

Sign up for the 1001 Dark Nights Newsletter
and be entered to win a Tiffany Key necklace.

There's a contest every month!

Go to www.1001DarkNights.com to subscribe.

As a bonus, all subscribers will receive a free
1001 Dark Nights story
The First Night
by Lexi Blake & M.J. Rose

One Thousand and One Dark Nights

Once upon a time, in the future…

*I was a student fascinated with stories and learning.
I studied philosophy, poetry, history, the occult, and
the art and science of love and magic. I had a vast
library at my father's home and collected thousands
of volumes of fantastic tales.*

*I learned all about ancient races and bygone
times. About myths and legends and dreams of all
people through the millennium. And the more I read
the stronger my imagination grew until I discovered
that I was able to travel into the stories… to actually
become part of them.*

*I wish I could say that I listened to my teacher
and respected my gift, as I ought to have. If I had, I
would not be telling you this tale now.
But I was foolhardy and confused, showing off
with bravery.*

*One afternoon, curious about the myth of the
Arabian Nights, I traveled back to ancient Persia to
see for myself if it was true that every day Shahryar
(Persian: شهريار, "king") married a new virgin, and then
sent yesterday's wife to be beheaded. It was written
and I had read, that by the time he met Scheherazade,
the vizier's daughter, he'd killed one thousand
women.*

*Something went wrong with my efforts. I arrived
in the midst of the story and somehow exchanged
places with Scheherazade — a phenomena that had
never occurred before and that still to this day, I
cannot explain.*

*Now I am trapped in that ancient past. I have
taken on Scheherazade's life and the only way I can
protect myself and stay alive is to do what she did to
protect herself and stay alive.*

*Every night the King calls for me and listens as I spin tales.
And when the evening ends and dawn breaks, I stop at a
point that leaves him breathless and yearning for more.
And so the King spares my life for one more day, so that
he might hear the rest of my dark tale.*

*As soon as I finish a story... I begin a new
one... like the one that you, dear reader, have before
you now.*

Chapter 1

You'd be really hot if you'd just lose some weight.

My fingers curled around my car keys as I stormed out of the bar and into the thick, muggy air of July. The jagged edges dug into my palm as I resisted the urge to walk back and shove the keys into one of the jackass's over-inflated muscles.

From the moment Rick asked me out, I knew the date was going to be a bad idea.

The second I'd stepped foot on the elliptical at the gym that was a part of the Lima Academy, I'd seen Rick buzzing from one chick to the next, wearing his nylon sweats and babyGap shirt, so tight I always expected it to burst at any given moment. I hadn't even realized he worked for Lima Academy until tonight, employed in their sales and marketing department, and I felt like I knew *everything* about him because that was all Rick did.

He talked about himself.

God, why did I even agree to go out with him? Was I that lonely and sad? The clicking of my heels across the sidewalk was my only answer. Parking in the city on a Friday night was ridiculous. It was going to take a year to get to my car.

You'd be really hot if you'd just lose some weight.

My lips thinned. I couldn't believe he actually said that to me, like it was a compliment. What in the actual hell? It wasn't like I didn't know I could stand to lose a few pounds or thirty, but in my twenty-eight years of life, I had long accepted that I would never, in the history of ever, have a thigh gap, my butt would always have strange dimples in it, and no amount of sit-ups were going to counterbalance my love of cupcakes.

Deep down, I knew why I agreed to go out with him. I hadn't been on a successful date in two years, and my last serious relationship had evoked the "to death do us part" clause.

I was twenty-eight.

A widow.

A twenty-eight-year-old widow who needed to lose weight.

Sighing, I turned the corner as I reached up, tucking my hair back from my face. A fine sheen of sweat dotted my brow. I stuck close to the edge of the sidewalk, walking under the street lamps and staying away from the dark shadows that bled out from the numerous alleys. I could see my car up ahead, at the end of the silent block. It was early for a Friday night, but I was going to go home, crack open that can of BBQ Pringles that had been calling my name all evening, and forget about Rick while diving into the latest Lara Adrian romance.

Why couldn't alpha vampires with a heart of gold be real?

A sudden pained grunt snagged my attention as I was halfway to my car. Instinct flared alive, a burning fire in my gut urging me to keep walking, but I looked to my right. I couldn't help it. My head turned on its own accord, a reflex, and I stumbled.

Horror seized me, freezing my muscles and shooting darts of ice through my blood. Terror slowed time, throwing the scene into stark detail.

Dull yellow light formed a halo over the three men in the alley. One stood further back from the other two. His hair bleached blond and greasy, sticking up all over his head. He had a scar. A thin slice across his cheek, paler than his skin. Another man was leaning against the brick wall of the building, crowding the alley. I couldn't make out his features, because his head was hanging from his shoulders, and he appeared barely able to stand, obviously injured. The other man, his head completely shaven, stood directly in front of the injured man, and even though I only saw his profile, it was a face I'd never forget.

Hatred bled into every line of the man's face, from the dark slash of brows and squinty eyes, to the hooked nose and distorted, curled upper lip. He was a big guy. Tall. Broad in the shoulders. He wore a white tank top, and as my gaze tracked down his arm, I could tell his skin was shadowed with markings. A tattoo. But I wasn't thinking about the tattoo when I saw what he held in his hand.

The bald man was pointing a gun at the injured man!

Instinct was screaming like a five-alarm fire. *Run. Get away. There's a gun! Go.* But I couldn't move, torn between shocked disbelief and some inherent, possibly suicidal urge to do the right thing, to intervene and to—

A small light burst and thunder cracked overhead. The injured man crumbled as if some grand puppeteer had cut his strings. He hit the ground with a fleshy smack, and for a moment, all I could hear was my heart beating fiercely, pushing blood through my veins.

That popping snap wasn't thunder. The burst of light was a spark.

Reality slammed into me as I stared at the fallen man in the alley. A dark puddle formed, spreading from where he lay face first on the dirty pavement. My heart seized in my chest as I opened my mouth, dragging in air.

No. No way.

The man with the scar was talking to the one with the gun, his voice an excited, high-pitched squeal, but I was beyond hearing the exact words. My hand spasmed, and the keys slipped from my grasp. They clattered off the sidewalk, as loud as me trying to run on a treadmill.

Bald man's head swung sharply in my direction, and if I had felt like time had slowed before, it stopped right then. Our gazes locked, and in an instant, a horrifying connection was formed. He saw me. I saw him.

I saw him shoot someone in *the face.*

And this man, this killer, knew that.

His arm started to lift. All my muscles reacted and unlocked at the same moment. Pulse pounding, I spun around and started running back toward the bar, my lungs burning as a scream tore out from me, a sound I was sure even in my darkest moments, I'd never made before.

Brick exploded to my left, showering wickedly sharp chunks into the air. Flashes of pain erupted along my cheek, and I stumbled. The heel on my shoe snapped and slipped off, but I kept running, leaving the shoe behind.

I needed to find someone. I needed to call for help. I needed—

Rounding the block, I slammed into someone. A startled scream was cut off as I bounced back. There was a grunt, and I felt a hand grasping for my arm, but it was too late. I went down, landing hard on my side. A flash of pain jarred my bones, knocking the air out of my lungs.

"Holy shit," a male voice boomed above me. "Are you okay?"

I gulped and wheezed air as I flopped onto my front as I heard a woman say, "Of course she's not okay, Jon. She kamikazed into you!"

Lifting my head, I peered through the hair that had fallen into my face. I saw them—the one with the scar and the bald man, the cold-blooded murderer, running away, down the sidewalk, beyond where my car was parked. I watched them until they disappeared.

"Miss?" the man asked. "Miss, are you okay?"

Hands shaking, I pushed up onto my knees. The whole world took on a startling clarity. Cars driving by sounded like airplanes. Nearby doors closing sounded as if they were being repeatedly slammed, and my own heart was beating like a steel drum.

"Yes. No." I rasped out. Pressing my fingers to my burning cheek, I jerked my hand back when I felt the wet warmth. Darkness smeared the tips of my fingers. My gaze shot back to where I'd run from. "We need to call the police. Someone has been shot."

Chapter 2

I'd never been inside a police station before. One might think I lived a boring life. No parking tickets to appear for. I'd never been fined for speeding. Even as a teenager, I obeyed the law.

Well, I did do a little underage drinking here and there, and I most definitely smoked a bit of weed in my day, but I'd never gone overboard.

And I'd been clever enough to not get caught.

But now I was sitting in one of those rooms that I'd only seen on reality TV. I was sure the camera in the corner wasn't for show. Although I'd done absolutely nothing wrong, I half expected a barrel-chested detective to burst through the door and start throwing accusations at me.

My fingers curled around the crumbled tissue I'd been holding for what felt like hours. The man I'd *kamikazed* into had called the police since I hadn't been able to figure out how to get my phone out of my purse and use it.

Shock.

That's what the EMTs who'd arrived right behind the flashing red and blue lights of the police cars had told me. They had wanted me to go to the hospital to get checked out, but the responding officers were understandably impatient. They needed answers. I was a witness to a—to a murder.

Because that man in the alley was dead.

And there was nothing seriously wrong with me. My palms were a bit raw and my body ached from my tumble. The cuts on my cheeks were nothing compared to what had happened to the man lying facedown in the alley.

I would be fine.

My breath caught, and I refused to close my eyes for anything longer than a second because when I had as the police officer drove me to the station, I saw the bald man firing the gun. I heard it crack. I saw the man fold like a paper sack.

I saw the bald man pointing the gun at me.

Terror resurfaced, and I shut it down before it took hold, but it was a struggle to not think about the fact that the murderer had seen my face. He knew that I was a witness. That was terrifying because there was no doubt in my mind that he would have no problem putting a bullet in me.

He had no problem doing it to that man.

Folding my arms across my chest, I stared at the near-empty paper cup in front of me. I'd all but gulped it down when the officer had brought it to me. A shiver rolled across my shoulders. It was so chilly in here. Even the tip of my nose was icy.

Instead of keeping my thoughts blank, I focused on what had happened. How much time I thought had passed between when I left the bar and had walked in front of the alley. What I saw was important. Someone was murdered, and I'd seen the persons responsible. Whatever information I had would help bring them to justice.

So I replayed the events over and over, up to the horrifying moment the gun had gone off, despite how badly it made me shudder and how I wished I had kept walking. That may be wrong, but I knew that until my dying day, I would never forget tonight.

That man died with his face pressed into an alley that smelled of urine.

I shuddered again. Never in a million years had I thought accepting a date with Rick the Dick would end with me sitting in a police station after witnessing…a murder.

I had no idea how long I'd been sitting in this room, but at some point an officer had shown up with my car keys. After confirming the make and model, the officer had left again to retrieve my car from the scene. I wasn't sure if that was protocol or not, but I appreciated the gesture.

The last thing I wanted to do was return to the scene.

A shaky breath puffed out as the door opened, causing my chin to jerk up. Two men entered. The first thing I noticed was that both were dressed like I expected detectives to be. The first man wore tan trousers and the other one had on black. The first man's dress shirt was slightly wrinkled, as if he had gotten the call in the middle of the night and had picked the first thing up from the floor. He was older, possibly in his fifties, and his dark gaze was sympathetic as he moved closer to the table. The scent of fresh coffee wafted from the cup he held. He placed a closed file on the table.

"Ms. Ramsey? I'm sorry to keep you waiting. I know you've had a long night. I'm Detective Hart." He stopped, turning halfway. "And this is Detective…"

I was already looking up at the other guy, taking in how the pressed, white polo was loose at his trim waist and a bit tighter along a clearly defined chest and shoulders. Right now really wasn't the best moment to be checking out a guy, so I forced myself to look up. My gaze had just moved to his face when Detective Hart introduced the second detective.

My heart stopped for the second time that evening.

Oh my God.

I could feel my eyes widen as I gawked at the second man, who was openly staring back at me with the same look of disbelief on his unbelievably handsome face. I didn't even need to hear his name spoken. I knew who it was.

Colton Anders.

Oh my God, there was no mistaking him. Those high, angular cheekbones, the cut line of an often stubborn jaw, his full lips and those bright and piercing blues eyes had spawned an embarrassing amount of fantasies in high school and beyond.

God, it probably made me a terrible person. I had a boyfriend all through high school—a boy who ultimately became my husband—but there had always been Colton. He was the untouchable god in high school, the boy you went to school for and lusted for from afar, even though an icicle had a better chance of surviving in hell than you did when it came to gaining his attention.

Colton was classically handsome, just like his younger brother, Reece, and he looked more ready to arrive at a fashion shoot for a men's health magazine than he appeared ready to investigate a homicide.

So shocked at the sight of him, the question blurted out of me. "I thought you worked for the county?"

"I did, but I transferred to the city." Colton lifted his arm, running his hand over his dark brown hair. Did he still live in Plymouth Meeting? Had he moved to Philadelphia? Those questions were so inappropriate, and I was amazed I kept my mouth shut as he stared at me. "Damn, Abby. I had no idea it was you in this room."

He knew my name? Let alone, remembered it? The Kool-Aid dude could burst through the one-way mirror and I wouldn't be any more surprised. Colton and I hadn't run in the same circles, and I was sure, a hundred percent positive, I hadn't been on his radar in high school.

"You two know each other?" Hart asked with a frown as he glanced between us.

Colton gave a tight shake of his head. "We went to high school together, but I haven't seen her..." He lowered his arm. "I haven't seen you in years."

Oh, but I had seen him around town. Not often. At the grocery store once in a while. Once at the movies. I'd been with my friend and he had been with this statuesque blonde.

"I..." Swallowing hard, I glanced at Detective Hart. Off kilter from what had happened, I already felt like I was stuck in a dream. Or a nightmare. "I left for college and then moved to New York after I graduated. I've been back for about four years."

Colton stepped around Hart and those blue eyes, framed by a heavy fringe of lashes, narrowed. "Are you okay?" His head jerked back toward the other detective. "Has she seen an EMT?"

"From what Officer Hun said, she was treated and refused to go to the hospital."

That narrowed gaze landed on me sharply. "You need to get—"

"I'm fine." How bad did my face look? I resisted the urge to glance at the one-way glass window. "Really, I am."

"You were shot at," Colton stated.

I flinched, unable to stop myself. Either the responding officer had filled him in or that info was in the file. "The bullet must've hit a nearby wall. It was chunks of brick." Pausing, I wetted my lips. "It's not…"

Colton's gaze dipped to my mouth for a second too long for me to have completely imagined it. His eyes met mine quick enough as he slid into the seat closest to me on my left. "Have you called your husband?"

What the…? I blinked once and then twice. He knew I'd married? Granted, it wasn't like it had been a secret or anything. Kevin and I…we'd gotten married right after graduation, during the summer, and by winter we had moved. Yes, we all went to school together, but I had been completely invisible to him.

Drawing in a shallow breath, I loosened my grip on the tissue as I refocused my thoughts. "Kevin passed away four years ago. It was a car accident."

"Shit." Colton straightened as the look in his steeling blue gaze softened. "I didn't know." He reached over, placing his large hand on my shoulder. The weight was shockingly comforting. "I'm sorry, Abby."

"It's…" It wasn't exactly okay even though I'd long come to terms with the loss of Kevin. Some days it was still hard. Something small, like a certain scent or a song on the radio would remind me of him and how uncertain life could be. "Thank you."

He squeezed gently and then lowered his hand, the tips of his fingers brushing the bare skin of my arm. "Okay. Let's get this over so you can go home."

Hart arched a brow as he eyed Colton. He took the seat across from me. "I know you've already given your statement to Officer Hun, but we're going to want you to start from the beginning, okay?"

I nodded slowly. "I was leaving the bar Pixie's and walking to my car. It was parked a couple of blocks away. Maybe three or four blocks. It was early. Maybe around eight-thirty. I was on a…a date, but the guy was a total douchebag." My cheeks heated as my gaze darted to Colton. "I'm sorry. That's not really important."

Colton's lips twitched. "Everything is important."

I forced myself to take another slow, steady breath. "All right. I was walking to my car and I really wasn't paying attention. That area of the city isn't bad and so I wasn't expecting anything to happen, you know? I was just walking and I saw my car up ahead. I was thinking about going home and reading this book," I continued, knowing I was rambling again. "I heard someone groaning and it was like I had no control over my feet. I stopped and I looked to my right. There was an alley and that's when I saw them."

Extending an arm, Colton snatched up the file on the table and flipped it open. His brows burrowed together as he quickly scanned it. "You said you saw three people."

"Yes. There was a man just standing there. He had...he had a scar on his face and bleached blond hair. The other man, the one with the gun, his head was shaven and he had a huge tattoo on his arm. I couldn't make out what it looked like. It was too dark. I'm sorry."

He glanced up at me, his gaze roaming over my face. "That's okay. You told the officer you could recognize them, right?" When I nodded again, he smiled tightly. Not the big, warm smile I'd seen him throw around when we were teenagers. Not even a hint of it. "They're compiling some mug shots of those who've met your description right now. So we'll go over that in a few." There was a pause as he sat back in the chair. "How many times did you hear the gun fire?"

"Once. No. Twice," I said. Detective Hart was scribbling something down on a small notebook he must've had hidden somewhere. "He shot...he shot that man in the alley, and I dropped my keys like a dumbass. Oh!" I smacked my hand over my mouth. "I'm sorry."

The blue hue of Colton's eyes had lightened. "Honey, saying dumbass around here isn't going to offend anyone."

"No truer words ever spoken," Hart added dryly.

The smile that curved up the corners of my lips felt weak and brittle. I'd also never in a million years thought I'd hear Colton call me honey. Hell, never in a million years did I think I'd be sitting in front of him.

I really needed to focus, but now it was a struggle. Adrenaline had long since faded and it was way past my normal bedtime of eleven-thirty. "Um, after I dropped the keys, the man with the gun, he turned to me. I saw him. He...he saw me." My fingers tightened around the poor tissue as a slice of panic cut across my chest. "I turned and ran. He must've fired at me, but missed. The bullet hit a nearby building." I raised my hand toward my cheek and then immediately dropped it back to my lap. "I kept running and that's when I ran into the man."

Detective Hart asked a few more questions. Did I notice if they had gotten in a car? No. Was a name even spoken? Not that I recalled. Did they say anything to the man they shot? I wasn't sure. Eventually, he got up and left the room to retrieve some photos they wanted me to look at.

I was alone with Colton.

Any other time I probably would've been beside myself with nervousness, but at this point, I barely registered his presence. All I wanted to do was go home and forget this night.

"Abby?"

My gaze slowly lifted at the sound of my name. His voice was deep and gruff—a morning voice.

He leaned toward me, placing his arms on the table. Short dark hairs dusted powerful forearms. The few times I'd seen him over the years, I hadn't been in close proximity to him, but now I could see the tiny differences between the Colton I'd admired from afar in high school and the one sitting in front of me, some ten years later. Fine lines had formed around the corners of his eyes. His jaw seemed harder, and the five-o'clock shadow was something new.

Something sexy.

I really needed to stop thinking in general.

"Are you sure you're okay, Abby?" he asked, and real concern filled his voice.

I shook my head slowly as a shiver raced down my spine. "Yes. No? I'm sorry. I'm so tired."

"I can imagine." He glanced at the door as he moved his shoulders, as if working out a kink. "We'll get you home soon."

Slouching in the metal chair, I sighed. "Is this…the start of your shift or…?"

Colton's cobalt gaze tracked back to me. "I usually get off around eight, but we work in cycles for homicide calls. It was our weekend."

"Sorry," I whispered, and then frowned. "I don't even know why I apologized. It's got to be hard working those kinds of hours, having to be on call."

"I imagine it is for some, especially those with a family." One side of his lips quirked up, and despite the dire situation, my stomach dipped a bit. He lifted his left hand. "Obviously, I'm not married. I wouldn't know."

I thought about the beautiful blonde I'd seen him with at the movies. "No girlfriend?" My eyes widened. Did I seriously just ask that?

That half grin spread, revealing the one dimple he had in his left cheek. "No. Not really."

Not really? What in the heck was that supposed to mean? Did it matter? No. Not at all. I dropped my gaze to the table. A moment passed and I didn't think about what I was saying. It just…came out. "I'd never seen anyone die before. Never saw the exact moment life was snuffed out. I'd lived through death. With my parents and then with Kevin, but…" I'd seen my husband after he'd passed away. He'd been a pale, waxy shadow of himself and as traumatizing as that was, it was nothing compared to witnessing a life end. "I won't ever forget tonight."

"You won't," he said, and I lifted my gaze to his. "I'm not going to lie to you. It's going to hang with you. Seeing death like that isn't easy. It's a darkness you just can't explain and can't understand."

That was so true. "You see it a lot?"

His head tilted to the side. "I've seen enough, Abby. Enough."

The need to apologize again rose, but I squelched it now. It was a terrible habit of mine. Apologizing for things I had no control over. Without apologizing, I had no idea what to say to him.

"I need to ask you one more time," he said, all softness gone from his eyes. They were like chips of blue ice. "Are you positive you didn't hear any of their names?"

"The one guy was talking—the one with the scar, but I didn't hear what he was saying. I was too…shocked by what I was seeing. I wish I did, but I couldn't make any of it out, but I got this impression that he…I don't know."

"What impression?" He leaned forward, gaze sharpening.

Unsure if what I was saying was correct or more of just a feeling, I squirmed a little in my chair. "I got this feeling that he wasn't okay with what was happening. He appeared upset. Like he had his hands in his hair. Like this." I raised my hands to my shoulder-length hair and scrubbed my fingers through it. "He seemed upset. I know that's not much—"

"No, that's definitely something. That's good."

"How?"

Colton smiled tightly. No dimple. "Because if this guy didn't like what was going down, then he could turn against the one who pulled the trigger."

"Oh." I thought that made sense.

He was quiet for a moment. "What a horrible way for you and I to run into each other again, huh?"

My answering smile didn't feel as forced as the one before. "Yeah. Not the greatest circumstances." I reached up, tucking my hair behind my ear. I started to yawn, weary with exhaustion, but the stretching of my face caused me to wince. "Ow."

Colton had somehow moved closer and before I knew it, I could catch the scent of his cologne. It was crisp, reminding me of mountain air. A single finger curved under my chin, startling me. The touch was simply electrifying, like a jolt of pure caffeine to the nervous system. The grasp was surprisingly tender. That softness was back in his gaze.

And it had been so long since I'd been touched in what felt like such an intimate way.

For some god-awful reason, tears started climbing the back of my throat. Granted, there were currently a lot of reasons to begin sobbing hysterically, but the last thing I needed to do was cry over Colton.

I knew I should pull away from him because the comfort his slight touch offered was too much. The wall I had built around the nearly consuming terror started to crumble. "That man…that murderer? He saw me," I repeated in a hushed voice. "If I can describe him, he can describe me." My voice caught, cracked a little. "That's terrifying."

"I know how scary that is, but trust me, Abby." The hard glint was back in his icy eyes as his hand shifted slightly and his thumb smoothed under the tiny cut along my cheek. "I'm going to make sure you're safe."

Chapter 3

None of the pictures that had been splayed out in front of me or had been included in the most disturbing photo album ever were of the men I'd seen in the alley.

Strangely, I felt like I had failed.

I wanted to be able to point at someone and say that was them. The bad guys would be found, and all of this would be over. I wanted that so badly.

But that was not what happened.

Colton had been called out toward the end and even though he'd said he'd be back, I hadn't seen him while I was ushered out of the police station and guided to my car by Detective Hart.

They'd be in touch.

I had no idea what that meant and I was too exhausted to figure it out. The drive from the city to the townhouse I'd purchased when I moved back wasn't particularly quick, even at damn near close to three in the morning. By some kind of miracle, I made it home, parked my car, and hobbled up the steps and let myself in. It was only then that I remembered that my one heel was broken. I didn't recall how I got the shoe back. Maybe Officer Hun?

Or was it Colton?

God.

Please not Colton.

I really didn't need him knowing that I was near caveman size when it came to my feet.

Flipping the light on inside, I quickly closed the door behind me and kicked off my ruined shoes. My pinched toes sighed in relief as I stared up at the narrow staircase directly in front of the door. More than anything I wanted to climb those steps and throw myself into my bed, but I felt disgustingly dirty and my throat felt like the Mojave Desert.

The section of townhouses had been built in the early nineties so the entire first floor rocked the whole open concept. The living room area was cozy with a couch and chair, situated around a TV and coffee table. The space opened right into a dining room that I honestly never used. Most of my dinners were on the couch. All the appliances had been new in the kitchen, and I'd fallen in love with the gray granite countertops the moment I walked into it.

I turned on the light in the kitchen and went straight to the fridge. Diets be damned. I picked up a can of Coke, popped the lid, and nearly drank all of it while the fridge door was still open, throwing out cold air.

"God," I whispered, lowering the can slowly as I closed the fridge door. "Tonight…"

There were no words.

I turned around and walked out of the kitchen, carrying my can of soda and purse with me. As I walked back through the dining area, my gaze fell over the framed photos nailed to the wall. When I moved in, it had taken me nearly two years to hang those portraits.

Some were easier than others. Like the picture of me and the girls from college, standing in Times Square, or the really terrible college graduation photo. For some reason, I ended up looking cross-eyed in it. Most people would want to hide the photo, but it made me laugh.

It had made Kevin laugh.

My gaze tracked over to the photo of my parents. It had been taken in their home, in the kitchen I'd grown up in. It had been Thanksgiving morning and Dad had snuck up on Mom, wrapping his arms around her waist from behind. Both were smiling happily.

They passed away in a car accident my second year of college. It had been a huge blow, shattering. Dealing with the loss of both parents at once had been nearly impossible, but naïvely, I had believed that would be the only real loss I'd suffer. I mean, come on, what was the statistical probability of losing another loved one to something as unfair and unpredictable as another car accident?

The only photo I had hanging of Kevin was the one of him standing alone at our wedding, dressed in the tux he'd rented from a cheap wedding shop in town. It was outside, in the bright July sun, and he was more golden than blond. I loved this photo so much because it captured the warmth in his brown eyes.

That was Kevin. Always warm. Always welcoming. He was the kind of person who never met a stranger. I pressed my lips together as I stared at his boyishly handsome face. As the months had turned into years, it became harder and harder to pull his features from memory alone. The same with my parents. There were days when all of them would appear in my mind as clear as day, while other days they were nothing more than a ghost.

I'd loved Kevin. I still did. And I missed him. We had been high school sweethearts, and he'd been the only man I'd been with. Looking back, I knew we didn't have the kind of passion that curled the toes or woke you up in the middle of the night, wet and ready, and we were simply...familiar with one another, but we loved each other.

And I didn't regret a second I spent with him.

I just regretted the moments afterward because I knew that Kevin would've wanted me to move on, to find someone else to love. He wouldn't want me to be alone.

My throat clogged and I briefly squeezed my eyes shut against the rush of tears. Holding it together, I trudged on, heading upstairs. There were three bedrooms, but one of them was barely large enough to hold a bed, so it had become my office. Which was perfect because the room faced the backyard and the garden down below, enabling me to procrastinate for hours when I should be working.

I passed the tiny hallway bedroom and entered the master at the front of the townhouse. The room was spacious, complete with its walk-in closet and attached master bath. The Jacuzzi tub had become my best friend forever since I moved in.

Flipping on the nightstand light, I walked my purse over to the dove-gray sitting chair near the door. I dug my phone out and then plugged it into the charger on the nightstand. All I wanted to do was plop face first onto the bed, but I went into the bathroom and peeled off my clothes. I started to dump them in the laundry basket, but instead, I rolled them up in a ball, panties and bra included, to take down to the trash in the morning. I didn't want to wear the clothing again, let alone see it.

Tired, I cranked the water up and waited with my back to the mirror above the sink for the water to heat up to near scalding temps, the way I liked it.

I tried not to look at myself in the mirror when I was completely nude.

I didn't like to see my reflection.

I wasn't...comfortable with it.

It wasn't the tiny dimples or the roundness of certain parts of my body that made me uncomfortable. It wasn't physical. Or maybe it was, because I hadn't felt...attached to my own skin in a while. I knew that sounded crazy, but it was almost like I no longer even knew my own body. It was something that I wore. I wasn't intimate with it beyond using my trusty vibrator every so often. Maybe I'd just gone too long without intimacy.

And tonight, for the first time in years, I actually felt *something* when Colton had touched my chin. And how sad was that? The guy had touched my chin and that was the closest to physical interaction I'd gotten since Kevin.

This was the last thing I wanted to think about tonight. My body ached as if I had overexerted myself as I stepped under the steady spray. The shower felt like the longest of my life and slipping on the worn Penn State shirt and thin, cotton shorts was literally a chore.

Finally, after what felt like forever, I was in bed, but I couldn't sleep. I stared at the silently spinning ceiling fan and I couldn't stop thinking about the man who died tonight. Did he have a family? A wife who was going to be getting that horrific knock on the door? Did he have kids? Were his parents still alive and would soon be burying their son? Would they ever catch the man responsible?

Did I have something to fear?

Reaching over, I picked up the remote and turned the TV on, keeping the volume low, but it did nothing to stop the steady stream of thoughts.

I'd seen someone die.

Squeezing my eyes shut, I rolled over onto my side and for the first time in years, I cried myself to sleep.

* * * *

The following morning, I stood directly in front of my coffee maker, bleary-eyed and impatient as I waited for pure happiness to stop percolating. All I'd managed to do so far was scoop up my hair and toss it up in a messy twist, but already, shorter strands were either slipping free or sticking out in every direction.

In other words, I looked like a hot mess, but I really didn't care as I poured the steaming coffee into a cup halfway full of sugar, and I still stood there, taking my first drink, my second, and my third as the cool tile seeped through my bare feet.

I'd overslept.

Well, sleeping past eight a.m. nowadays was sleeping in. It was close to nine before I dragged myself out of bed. It wasn't that big of a deal. The only thing I had planned later in the day was to meet up with Jillian Lima for dinner.

Jillian and I met each other at a book signing in the city. She was almost ten years younger than me, but the age difference had quickly evaporated. Jillian was a hard cookie to crack. She was almost debilitating shy, but love of books crosses all barriers. We bonded over our favorite authors and themes, and once she discovered what I did for a living, she started to open up.

For the last year, we met every Saturday night to discuss books over dinner. Sometimes we'd grab a movie or head to the bookstore, and I was going to miss her. In the spring, she would be transferring to a college in West Virginia. I still didn't know why she was doing that. That was a little nugget of info I couldn't wiggle out of her.

I'd just topped off my cup of coffee when the doorbell rang, surprising me. I wasn't expecting anyone. Leaving the cup on the counter, I padded across the floor and peered out the front window, but since there were always cars I didn't recognize parked out front, that made no difference. Rolling my eyes, I reached for the door handle, cursing the fact that there wasn't a peephole in the door.

My jaw unhinged on a sharp inhale, and the ability to form comprehensive thoughts fled.

Colton Anders, in all his blue-eyed babe glory, stood on my stoop. "Good morning, Abby."

Chapter 4

I was beyond responding.

He stood there with a medium-size pink box in one hand and the other shoved in the pocket of his trousers. The five-o'clock shadow was heavier, giving him a rough edge that my sleep-fogged mind found incredibly sexy.

Okay. I would find that sexy anytime.

Any. Time.

He was dressed as he was the night before, and I had the distinct impression he hadn't been to bed yet, which really wasn't fair, because how could he look *this* good without sleeping?

One side of his lips curled up, revealing the left-sided dimple. "Can I...come in? I brought crepes with me."

I blinked.

"You like crepes, right? You have to like them," he added, grinning. "Everyone loves crepes and these are the shit. They are rolled in cinnamon and brown sugar."

"I...I thoroughly enjoy them." My ass also thoroughly enjoyed them. Moving back, I stepped aside. "How do you know where I live?"

Colton stepped in, his chin dipped down. I wasn't a small lady, coming in at five foot eight, but standing next to him, I felt small, delicate even, and that was an odd feeling. "It was on your statement. I probably should've called first, but I was on my way home from the station and your house was on the way. So was the bakery."

I didn't know what to say as I closed the door behind him, but my heart was pounding in my chest and my stomach was wiggling in a weird way, sort of like the way I'd seen described a thousand times. Butterflies. But more powerful. Like large birds of prey or pterodactyls. "You live nearby?"

His grin spread. "I live over on Plymouth Road."

That was nowhere near my house. The butterflies increased. "Oh. In the apartments over there?"

He nodded. "Did I wake you?"

"No. I..." That was about when I realized that I was wearing nothing but a pair of sleep shorts and an old shirt that pretty much hid nothing. I didn't even need to look down to know that my nipples were most likely noticeable. And my thighs? Oh, dear God.

My hair.

"I smell coffee though," he said, glancing toward the kitchen. "So I'm guessing not?"

He spoke as if he hadn't noticed I had some major headlights and chub rub going on, but then again, why would someone like Colton even notice that in the first place? My attention flipped to the stairway. A huge part of me wanted to rush upstairs and throw a Snuggie on. Or at least a bra.

I really needed to put a bra on.

"No. You didn't wake me up," I said, glancing back at him. The air suddenly punched out of my lungs.

Colton was so not looking at my face.

He was looking below the shoulders, his gaze lingering in some areas longer than others. Like at the edge of my shorts and then across the chest, as if he were committing the words Penn State to memory. A tingle buzzed to the tips of my breasts. His gaze gradually drifted up to my face and those blue eyes...they reminded me of the core of a flame. Heat blossomed deep inside me, infiltrating my veins. The intensity of it was shocking.

So much so I stepped back. "I'm going to...I'll be right back."

That half grin remained in place. "Mind if I help myself to the coffee?"

"No. Not at all." I edged toward the stairwell. "Help away."

Spinning around, I dashed up the stairs and into my bedroom. Once inside, I pressed my palms to my warm cheeks. "Oh my God."

I headed into the bathroom and saw, thank God, that my face wasn't blood red, but my cheeks were flushed and my hazel eyes, more brown than green, seemed bright. Feverish. Turning on the cold water, I bent over and quickly splashed it over my face. Oh goodness, I had only ever read about men staring at women in a way that it felt like a physical touch before. I hadn't really believed it possible.

It was.

Straightening, I grabbed my toothbrush and quickly got down to business, all the while trying to get a grip on reality. It didn't take a genius to figure out that Colton was here because of what happened last night. There could be no other reason, so I needed to keep my overactive imagination where it belonged, at work. Yes, it was odd that he'd just pop over, but maybe he felt like he needed to tell me in person. And the checking me out? Maybe he was just reading my shirt.

Okay. That was stupid. He had definitely been looking at my breasts, but he was a dude and I was a chick, so these things happened.

Especially when you were nipply and you weren't wearing a bra.

I grabbed a bra and a pair of yoga pants I'd never in my entire life ever worn while doing yoga. I quickly re-twisted my hair and then resisted the urge to put makeup on. At this point, if I went back downstairs with a peachy glow and to die for lashes, it would be way too obvious.

I couldn't believe Colton Anders had seen me braless before I had my first full cup of coffee. What is my life?

Ugh.

Ignoring the near constant flutter in the pit of my stomach, I headed back downstairs. What I saw had the weirdest, bittersweet feel to it.

Colton had placed the box of crepes on the dining table and moved my cup of coffee to the seat catty-corner to where he was sitting, at the head of the table. A fresh cup of coffee was placed in front of him. There were even plates and he'd found my napkins. And utensils.

It was so…familiar, and again, intimate.

"How are you hanging in there after last night?" he asked without looking up.

"Okay, I guess. I mean, I'm trying not to think about it." Except that was a terrible lie. It was almost all I thought about last night.

He glanced up and the side of his lips quirked up. "I must say, I sort of liked what you were wearing before more."

My cheeks flushed red as I made my way to the table. "You must be exhausted then."

One eyebrow arched. "Oh, sweetheart, I'm never too tired to appreciate the beauty of a woman who just woke up and is still walking around in the clothes she slept in."

I sat down, eyeing him like he was a foreign species. "I didn't know you were a charmer."

"More like an outrageous flirt," he corrected, opening the box of crepes. "Obviously I'm not very good at it."

Clasping my hands in my lap, all I could do was watch him pluck up a crepe and plop it down on my plate. Was he saying he was trying to flirt with me? That was definitely not typical detective protocol.

Well, not outside romance novels.

"I'm still shocked that it was you when I walked into the office last night. God. How many years has it been? Too many." He moved on, picking up another crepe and placing it on his plate. "I really am sorry to hear about Kevin. The one thing I've learned over and over is that life is not guaranteed. Ever."

"That's true." I glanced at the crepe. It looked delish, but nerves were conquering my appetite. "It's hard to deal with and move on, but you do, even when there are a lot of moments when you don't think that'll happen."

"And you have?" He picked up a knife and fork, cutting into the crepe. "You've moved on?"

"I..." The question caught me off guard, and I glanced at the photo of Kevin. "It was four years ago and I...I will always love him, but I have...I have closed that chapter of my life."

His gaze flicked to mine and he didn't look away as he lifted a piece of crepe to his mouth. He ate it with pure enjoyment, as if it was the first and last piece of food he'd ever devoured, and I couldn't help but think if he ate food with such gusto, what he was like eating—

I cut that thought off and quickly turned my attention to my plate.

Oh my God, what was wrong with me? Why I was thinking about Colton eating...well, definitely not food. Then again, who wouldn't think about that when they saw him and those lush lips?

"So what have you been up to, Abby?"

My chin jerked up as my heart turned over heavily. "I graduated from Penn State. Um, I worked in New York at a publishing house."

His brows flew up. "Really? That's impressive."

I shrugged a shoulder. "Well, it was not an easy job to get. I had to put my time in. Luckily, I was able to spend a summer interning while in college. It helped open connections, but I was still an assistant editor by the time I left. Kevin worked at a different publishing house. He made senior editor in record time. Of course."

"Why?" He was almost done with his crepe.

I smiled faintly. "The publishing industry sure loves their boys."

"Interesting. I didn't know that." He paused. "And you left after Kevin passed away?"

I nodded. "I just...well, I wasn't a fan of the city. Even Philadelphia has nothing on New York. It was so damn expensive and I didn't see a point in staying there afterward."

He picked up a second crepe. "And do you still work as an editor?"

"Freelance." I reached up, tugging a strand of hair that came loose back and behind my ear. "I still freelance for publishers and for indies."

"Indies?" Genuine curiosity colored his tone.

"Independent authors—those who don't work with a publisher. Right now I'm working on Jamie McGuire's new novel. It's called *Other Lives*, and it's freaking fantastic. Sometimes my job is hard, though."

"Why? Dealing with authors?"

I laughed. "All the authors I've worked with have been great. Like Jamie? She's one hell of a firecracker, but she's a sweetheart. But sometimes I just suck at remembering this is a job. Like I need to be paying close attention, but I get caught up in the story and the next thing I know I have to go back and reread an entire chapter. I'm hoping she hires me for her next Maddox Brother's book. I'm a huge..." I laughed, a bit self-consciously. "Sorry. I can be a bit of a fan girl."

"It's okay."

I bit down on my lip. "There's nothing more amazing than seeing a book you've worked on get talked about and loved or when it hits a list. You feel like you're a part of something bigger."

Colton was grinning as he watched me closely. "You really love your job."

"I love books," I said simply. "There's nothing more powerful than the written word. It can transfer you to a place that exists right now that you'll never get to visit or it can take you to a world that doesn't. It can show you things you'll never experience otherwise in life, and books…most importantly, they can take you out of your own world, and sometimes you need that."

"I feel you." He was still watching me with those intent blue eyes.

A moment of silence passed between us. "I'm sure you didn't come here to hear about all of that."

He put his fork down. "Actually, yeah, I did."

I blinked. "What?"

Colton leaned toward me with his gaze locked onto mine. "I didn't know you in high school, but I knew of you."

"You did? I can't imagine it was anything interesting. I was boring as—"

"I never got the impression you were boring," he interrupted, and goodness, I could fall into those eyes and never come back out. So cheesy sounding, and if I saw it in one of my author's books, I'd redline the hell out of that, but now I got it. It was possible. "I just thought you were this pretty girl who sat two seats behind me in history class and was shy."

Several things occurred to me at once. He remembered that we shared history class together? Holy crap on a cracker. And he thought I'd been pretty? I was sure I probably weighed twenty pounds more back then and I wore these god-awful glasses that were so trendy nowadays.

Colton *was* a flirt.

"Looking back, I wish I had the balls to talk to you then." He returned his attention to his crepe while my jaw hit the table. "But you were with Kevin and…yeah, that's not my style, you know?" He glanced in my direction. "You're going to eat the crepes, right?"

"Yeah," I murmured, cutting into one side. I forced myself to eat a bite, and it was like heaven just orgasmed in my mouth. Wow. That was inappropriate. I resisted a giggle. "What about you? You've been a cop this whole time?"

"Yep. It's what I always wanted to do. Started off as a deputy, then became a detective for the county before transferring to the city. I love working as a detective, but with my hours all over the place, Reece, my brother, has pretty much straight up adopted my dog. She doesn't even stay at my house anymore." He finished off the second crepe with an impressive quickness and then settled back against the chair, stretching out his long legs. "Almost got married."

Thank God I had just swallowed a piece of crepe because there was a good chance I would've choked. "Almost?"

"Was engaged." He grinned, and I felt my tummy dip in response. "Nicole and I were together for...hell." He glanced up at the ceiling, pursing his lips. "For about six years."

Holy crap, six years? That was a long time. I wondered if she was the woman I'd seen him with at the movies that one time, but that was like, maybe a year ago.

"Got all the way down to planning the wedding date when we came to the realization that we wanted different things in life."

I picked up my coffee, more intrigued than I should be, but I couldn't imagine what more this mystery woman could've wanted beyond having Colton putting a ring on it. Granted, there was more to life, to a relationship, than having a hot guy to wake up to, but Colton and his younger brother, Reece, had always given the good-guy vibes. Colton could've changed since high school, but I didn't think so. "How so?"

"At first I think Nicole liked the idea of dating a cop." He laughed as he ran his finger along the rim of his cup, and damn, he had long fingers. "But it's not an easy life. Odd hours. Then there's the danger factor. I make decent money, but I'm never going to be rolling around in it. I think she hoped that I'd grow tired of being a cop."

I didn't understand. "But you guys were together a long time. Why would she think it was something you'd grow tired with?"

He raised a shoulder. "I think some people pretend at being okay with something because they think there's some kind of payoff in the end. That they'll eventually get what they want, and when they realize that's never going to happen, they just can't pretend anymore."

I shook my head. "I still don't get it. Why would someone waste their time pretending—waste the other person's time? There's no point in pretending in a relationship. It'll never work."

His dark lashes lowered, shielding his eyes as a small smile played across his lips. "Agreed."

Sipping my coffee, I tried to ignore the wild fluttering and the thousand questions whirling around in my head. I peeked over at him as I lowered my cup, and our gazes locked. Air leaked out of my parted lips. Colton didn't look away, and neither could I. Absolutely struck helpless by the intensity in his stare, the wisps of excitement building in my belly gave way to a slow burn that got my pulse pounding. How could a single look from him draw such a response? That gaze of his dipped, and I drew in a shallow breath and felt the warmth travel through my veins. Was he looking at my mouth again? Oh Lord, it was getting hot in here.

Goodness, this man…even his stare was pure…pure sin.

I cleared my throat. "So…um, when did you and Nicole part ways?"

"About six months or so ago."

Ice chased away the warmth as I schooled my expression blank. Six months? That wasn't a long time ago, especially considering they were engaged to be married and were together for six years. Six months was…was nothing. After I lost Kevin, six months had changed nothing for me. How could he be over the failure of a relationship in six months?

And why did it matter? No, it didn't, but there was no mistaking the rise of disappointment. I wanted to smack myself.

Colton leaned forward. "I did have another reason for stopping by. It's about what happened last night."

"Of course," I murmured, slapping a smile across my face as another surge of dismay made itself known.

He looked at me strangely. "I don't want to go into the gory details—"

"I can handle them." Or at least I thought I could. I was pretty sure I could.

That half smile was back. "When I got called out when I was talking with you, it was because the coroner had picked up the…body and had some evidence. Obviously, we know what the cause of death is, but I wanted to stop by and let you know that we are probably going to have an ID sometime today."

"Oh." I took a drink of my now lukewarm coffee.

"I also want you to contact me immediately if you see anything weird, okay?" Reaching into his pocket, he pulled out a business card and placed it on the table.

My gaze fell to the card. So formal. "What could be weird?"

"Just if you notice anyone hanging around here that you're not familiar with. Anything that gives you a bad vibe. That sort of thing."

I glanced up at him, the unease from earlier returning. "Should I be worried?"

"No." The smile he gave me this time didn't reach his eyes. "Just careful."

That really didn't make me feel warm and fuzzy, but couldn't he have just called me? If he had my address, then he had my cell.

The smile transformed and his face softened. "Yeah, I could've called you and told you that."

My chin jerked up as I almost dropped my cup. "Can you read minds? Oh man, I hope not."

His gaze did that slow slide again. "Now I'm curious to what I'd discover if I could read your mind."

I widened my eyes and said nothing because seriously, my mind was one step from face planting in the gutter when he was around.

Reaching over, he tapped his fingers on my arm. "I didn't want to just call you."

"Oh," I repeated. Goodness, I had this conversation thing down pat. It wasn't my fault. The tapping of his fingers had sent a fine shiver up my arm.

"And I was in the mood for crepes," he continued. "And when you're in the mood for crepes, you want to share them with a pretty lady."

My mouth opened but there were no words.

He chuckled as he rose. "I have to get going."

"Okay," I murmured, putting my cup on the table. I stood, following him to the door, and when he stopped suddenly, I nearly bounced off his back. His playful grin once again made an appearance. "Sorry."

Colton tilted his head to the side. "I'll be in touch, Abby."

As he left and I closed the door behind him, I leaned forward, gently knocking my forehead against it as I tried to stop my wayward thoughts from making a bigger deal out of his visit than I should.

But it was hard.

"Ugh." I pressed my forehead against the door and groaned.

Colton was an admitted flirt—an outrageous one. That was what he had to be doing because there was no way that it could be anything else. After all, how could it? Not when he was engaged six months ago, and he hadn't said who ended the relationship.

Besides, I wasn't his type. I wasn't cutting myself short by acknowledging that. Colton was...he was gorgeous. The kind of masculine beauty that could grace the covers of the books I edited, and he was also sweet—charming, and from what I remembered, intelligent to boot. And me?

I was the kind of woman who got the guy in the books.

But not in real life.

Never in real life.

Chapter 5

"Oh my gosh, that is so scary." Jillian brushed the heavy fringe of dark brown bangs out of her wide brown eyes. "Are you okay?"

"I'm fine." A little concealer had covered the tiny cuts on my face, and the palms of my hands only stung every so often. "It was scary and so unexpected."

"Who would expect that? Ugh." Jillian glanced down at her empty plates. We'd demolished our dinner and then our cheesecakes. "I can't even imagine. I probably would've run screaming and flailing in the other direction."

"That's pretty much what I did." I eyed the tiny crumb of cake on my plate and wondered how gluttonous I'd be if I ate that last piece.

"And that's probably why you're alive," she replied. "Even my father would have a hard time justifying a fight strategy rather than a flight one."

Jillian's father owned Lima Academy, and the sprawling building in downtown Philadelphia was more than just a gym. It was one of the premier mixed martial arts training facilities in the world. Jillian's father, skilled in his native Brazilian jiu jitsu, could've probably used his ninja stealth and taken the guys out with his karate skills.

"Speaking of your father, how is he handling the idea of you leaving in the spring?" I asked, changing the subject.

She cringed as she leaned back against the booth, folding her arms across her chest. Tension seeped into her pretty features. "He's still not exactly thrilled about it. He doesn't like the idea of me not being within his eyesight. Like something's going to…" She trailed off, shaking her head. "Anyway, do you still want to go to that signing Tuesday night?"

"Tiffany King's signing? Hell yeah." I relaxed when a genuine smile crossed her face. Conversations about her dad were usually a dead end. "She's going to be signing *A Shattered Moment*."

Jillian knocked her bangs out of her face. "I loved that book. Isn't there going to be another author with her, though?"

"Yeah, I think Sophie Jordan and Jay Crownover are going to be there." I glanced over at the couple walking past our table. "You want to meet at the bookstore?"

She nodded as she picked up her glass. "So," she drew the word out. "This Colton guy you mentioned? You went to high school with him?"

I bit back a sigh. I didn't know why I even brought him up, but I had, and I was woman enough to admit that I wanted to obsess over every little thing he'd said to me, but all I managed was a tight nod.

Jillian turned her head to the side and shot me a sidelong glance. "You know, when you brought him up earlier, you blushed."

"I did not."

"Yes, you did."

My eyes narrowed, but I laughed because yeah, I probably did. "I had the biggest crush on him in high school, and I know that's terrible because I was with Kevin and that probably makes me a terrible person."

"No, it doesn't." She rolled her eyes. "Just because you were with someone doesn't mean you're blind to everyone around you."

"True." I paused. "And Colton was hot."

Jillian giggled. "Was?"

"And now he like puts an extra 'o' and 't' in hot. He…he actually remembered me. Like he knew what class we shared."

Her brows rose, disappearing under her bangs. "Really?"

I nodded as I scrunched my nose. "And I think he was flirting with me. Okay. He was definitely flirting with me, but I think he's just a flirt. And guys who are flirts will flirt with anyone." I paused. "I wonder how many times I can say 'flirt' in a sentence?"

Jillian gave a close-lipped smile. "Oh, I know all about guys who will flirt with anything that's breathing." She glanced over at the empty table.

"Anyway, maybe he's interested."

"Ah, I don't know about that." Caving in, I scooped up the last little crumb of cake.

She frowned. "Why? You're smart and funny. You're pretty, and you love books. Why wouldn't he be interested?"

"Thanks," I laughed. "But he was engaged up until six months ago."

"Oh." Her lips pursed.

"And I'm not judging the fact he was in a previous serious relationship because so was I, but..." I stopped myself, laughing again. "Why am I even thinking about it in that kind of manner? I saw him last night because he's the detective investigating a homicide I witnessed and he stopped by this morning." I shook my head, clearing those thoughts away. "I don't even need to think about this in that way."

"I don't know," she replied after a moment. "But this whole thing sort of reminds me of a romance trope."

Another laugh burst out of me. "It sure does, except in real life, it never works out that way."

The truth was, even though that kind of thing only ever happened in books, I secretly dreamed of it happening to me. Sort of like a grown version of a girlie fantasy.

She shrugged as a far-off look appeared in her gaze and her response was soft. "I don't know about that. I like to believe—I need to believe— that happily ever afters exist in real life too." In that moment, she suddenly looked far older than nineteen. "For all of us."

* * * *

After dinner, I stopped at the grocery store in town, picking up a couple of necessary work items.

Coffee.

5-hour Energy drinks.

Skittles.

Chocolate.

Coke Zero.

Without these things, I was pretty much useless when it came to editing. When I worked in New York, I had a drawer in my desk full of three of those five things.

Checking out was a breeze and as I headed back into the waning daylight, I stowed the shopping cart and held on to my bag and case of soda with a death grip. Even though it was Saturday night, I would be working once I got my butt home and into comfy sweats. Working from home meant I kept weird hours.

Or in other words, I simply worked nearly every day.

I most definitely worked more now than when I traveled into an office every day. Then it had been easier to separate home from work. Not so much now.

As I neared my car, my steps slowed. When I'd gone into the store, the parking space beside my car had been empty, and I'd walked past plenty of vacant spaces on my way in and out, but now there was a van parked on my driver's side.

Not just any van. The creepy, white with no windows, kidnapper-type van.

My stomach dipped as I stopped a few feet from the van. Maybe I was just being paranoid after last night. Or maybe it had to do with Colton's warning about paying attention to anything weird, but either way, a tiny ball of dread had formed in the pit of my stomach.

The bag was starting to cut into my fingers and the case of cola was getting heavy. What could I do? Drop my groceries and run? Call Colton because there was a creeper van parked next to mine?

God, I watched way too much Investigation Discovery channel.

Then, before I could make up my mind to do anything, the passenger door creaked open and a male stepped out. My heart plummeted. He didn't look like he belonged stepping out of a work van. No way, no how. I wasn't trying to be judgie-mc-judgers, but his dark trousers, tucked in dark blue shirt, and polished dress shoes did not fit the rusted, broken-down creeper van.

Dark sunglasses obscured his eyes, but I had the distinct impression he was staring at me. Probably because I was standing there like an idiot, but then again, at this time of day, I couldn't figure out why he needed sunglasses. Ignoring the shiver slithering down my spine and the numbness in my fingers, I started walking again, fully prepared to turn the bag of groceries into a deadly weapon.

"It's a nice night, isn't it?" the man called out.

My aching fingers tightened around the strap of the plastic bag. I didn't smile. I didn't reply. The creep factor was off the charts, and as I neared the back of the van, I gave it a wide berth, ready for a posse of insane clowns to jump out and try to kidnap me.

Of course, the doors didn't open. I was going to walk to the passenger side and try to see if there was anyone else in the van before I went to the driver's door. Sounded legit.

"Your name is Abby, right?" the man said.

The air froze in my lungs, like I'd walked into subzero temperatures. Tiny hairs all along my body rose as if an army of cockroaches was running loose on my skin. I looked over my shoulder at him.

He stood by the back of his van with a close-lipped smile. A cold one. Predatory. "The Abby Ramsey, born and raised in Plymouth Meeting? Married her high school sweetheart who tragically passed away in a car accident about four years ago? The same Abby Ramsey who works from home as a freelance editor?"

Holy shit.

Holy shit balls on Sunday.

"Yeah, that's you," he continued. "You saw something last night that we need to chat about."

Talking was the last thing we needed to do. My heart pounded in my chest as I faced him. Why did the parking lot seem so empty now? It wasn't. People were milling around, but no one was paying attention to us. My gaze darted to the entry of the grocery store, trying to determine the distance if I had to make a run for it.

I wasn't much of a runner.

He took a step forward, and I blanched, lifting the heavy bag, prepared to swing if he got any closer. He raised his hands. "I'm not going to hurt you."

Famous last words. "Don't come any closer to me."

"I'm not. We can have our little conversation from a distance if that makes you happy." He smiled again, but it was chilling. "All I need you to understand, and I need you to really get this, is that you're not going to be able to identify anyone from last night."

An icy knot balled in my stomach.

"That's all, and that's not a big deal, is it? Just keep your mouth shut from here on out and nothing bad will happen. And you don't want anything bad to happen, do you?"

I was beyond responding, my heart thumping heavily in my chest. That was a threat, a very thinly veiled threat. Part of me couldn't believe this was happening.

"We want to make sure you keep your mouth shut," he said in the same friendly, conversational tone. "And I think you'll understand fairly quickly how serious we are."

Just then, the passenger window rolled down and all I saw was an arm extend out. A hand popped the side of the van, causing my heart to jump. The man backed up then, clapping his hands together as he said, "Now you have a nice evening."

I didn't move as he walked back to the van and climbed in. I didn't move when the old thing hunkered to life or when it pulled straight through the empty spot in front of it, turning left to head out of the parking lot.

"Oh my God," I whispered.

In a daze, I shoved my groceries into the trunk of my car with jerky, quick motions, and then I climbed in behind the wheel. I didn't even think for one second about what to do next. There was no way I was not going to call the police. Forget that. Before I left for dinner, I had shoved Colton's card in my purse. My mind raced. It made sense to call him because he knew what was going on. Calling 911 meant I'd have to tell them everything all over again.

As I pulled my cellphone out of my purse with a shaky hand, its unexpected shrill ring startled a tiny shriek out of me. Jesus. I looked down at the screen. It was a local number I didn't recognize. Normally I wouldn't answer, but for some unknown reason, this time I did.

I placed it to my ear and croaked out, "Hello?"

"Abby?"

My free hand landed on the steering wheel. I recognized the voice immediately. "Colton? I—"

"Thank fucking God you answered," he said, cutting me off. "Where are you?"

I blinked slowly, completely thrown off. "I'm...I'm sitting in the parking lot of the grocery store near…near Mona's."

"I want you to listen to me, okay?" There was the sound of a car door slamming and an engine keying on. "I want you to go inside and stay there, okay. Do not go home."

Chapter 6

I had kind of done what Colton had demanded. I'd gone into the grocery store and waited near their pharmacy, and when I spotted Reece, his younger brother, prowling through the sliding doors, I knew something really bad had happened.

Reece, a deputy with the county sheriff's office, had been in his uniform. I saw Reece around town a lot and knew he was seriously dating one of the bartenders over at Mona's, a girl we'd gone to school with, but for him to be the one to show up sent a chill over me.

"Something has happened at your house," he'd said, and that was all he would tell me.

He was supposed to wait with me until Colton could get from the city, but I wasn't having that. How could he just say something had happened at my house and then just expect me to stand around and wait? That was my *home*. After much arguing and more than a handful of concerned looks shot in our direction, Reece agreed—or relented—to escort me home.

Stars had started to dot the sky as we walked outside, all the while Reece muttering, "Colton's going to kick my ass."

One look at Reece told me that would be easier said than done. Yeah, Colton had an inch or two on him when it came to height, but Reece could hold his own.

In his county cruiser, he'd led me the short distance to my house. My hands had ached the entire drive and the moment I pulled into my parking space, I'd wanted to cry.

I hadn't.

Not when I'd climbed out of the car and saw the two officers standing by my open front door. I hadn't cried when I saw the shattered front window. And right now, as I stepped around Reece and went inside, I couldn't let the weight of everything that had happened in the last twenty-four hours get to me.

The TV, which sat near the window, was knocked over, shattered on the floor. Lying next to it was a huge cement block. I had no idea how someone could throw that thing through a window.

"Nothing else appears damaged," Reece said when I looked over at him. His hands rested against his duty belt. "But we're going to need you to look around to make sure nothing has been stolen."

Drawing in a shaky breath, I nodded as I tried to process what I was seeing. There was no way this wasn't related to what happened last night or the smarmy guy outside of the grocery store, but I still had a hard time believing it. Not because I was ignoring the evidence right in front of my face.

"Both the neighbors on either side of your townhouse weren't home," Reece explained. "No one else heard anything. When your neighbor on the right came home and saw it, she immediately called the police."

I needed to thank Betty, the elderly woman he must've been referencing. Coming home to this, on top of everything else, would've been horrifying.

"Are you okay, Abby?" Reece asked, stepping closer. "I know it can be hard to deal with the fact someone has done something like this to your house."

"I imagine you see this a lot, huh?" I worked my fingers together, hoping to ease the blood flow back in them as another officer scooped up the heavy cement brick with gloved hands. Something occurred to me right then. "How did Colton know about this?" This was so not his jurisdiction.

Reece watched the other officer carry the block out of the house. "He mentioned what happened last night when I saw him this afternoon—he mentioned you." A half grin appeared, nearly identical to Colton's. "Which is odd because he normally doesn't talk about witnesses or the fact that he shared crepes with one this morning."

My hands stilled and my eyes widened.

"I was the second officer to respond," Reece continued, the smile slipping away. "Once the neighbor next door said your name, I called Colton."

Was that allowed? I didn't know. Suddenly bone weary, I walked over to the chair and sat down, exhaling heavily. Over the years, since Kevin's death, I had learned how to deal with things. Last night, I had let myself have that little breakdown. It was understandable. I'd been a witness to a murder. If you were going to flip out about something, that was high up on the list of things to freak out over. But I needed to get it together now. I wasn't a shrinking violet, nor was I someone prone to hysterics.

The responding officer came in and I answered all his questions. When had I left the house? Where had I been? When I told them about stopping at the grocery store and the subsequent creeper dude in the creeper van, Reece snapped to attention.

"Why didn't you say something at the store?" he demanded, his eyes sharpening as he reached for his phone in his pocket.

"Um, I was kind of distracted by the dire message of not going home," I said. "But I'm telling you now."

Reece opened his mouth but seemed to rethink what he was saying. "I'll be right back." Stepping outside, I saw him lift his phone.

I wasn't sure how much time passed before I got up and accomplished what Reece had suggested. I checked everywhere, concentrating on my office and my bedroom. Nothing of any value was missing, which is what I told Reece when he appeared in my room.

I knew what the brick through the window was.

A message.

As I stood in front of my untouched jewelry box, I shuddered. Message was received, but that didn't mean I was going to listen. I'd already told the one officer and Reece, and I would tell Colton.

"Abby?" a deep voice boomed from downstairs. "Reece?"

I turned at the sound of Colton's voice and Reece's answering, "We're up here."

A handful of seconds later, Colton appeared in the doorway. He had changed since this morning, wearing a different police-issued polo. His blue eyes were fastened on me as he stepped into the bedroom.

"Are you okay?" he asked.

"She's okay," Reece answered, and then rolled his eyes when Colton shot him a look.

"I'm fine," I insisted, smoothing my hands along my skirt. "I'm just shook up."

Colton crossed the room and within a heartbeat, he was standing right in front of me. One hand curled around the back of my neck in a familiar, comforting gesture. The other landed on my shoulder. Our eyes locked, and my lips parted.

"The man at the store, he didn't harm you or anything?" he demanded, his gaze intently searching mine.

"No," I whispered, swallowing hard. "He just told me that I…I needed to keep my mouth shut. That I better not identify anyone from last night. And then he said that I'd understand quickly how serious the message is."

A muscle flexed along Colton's jaw as his gaze swept over my face. "Why didn't you call me?"

"I was going to. I was picking up my phone to call you, but you called me first. I was so caught off guard by what was happening here that I focused on that," I explained.

His hand tightened along the nape of my neck. It wasn't a constrictive or threatening move. It was one that was oddly tender. Intimate. Way beyond what he had to do, as a member of law enforcement, to comfort me.

The moment, whatever was going on between us, stretched out. There was something there, a jolt. Like touching a live wire. He sucked in an audible breath. His fingers spread along my shoulder, and the sudden urge to obliterate the tiny distance between us, to press my body against his, rode me hard. Without thinking, I stepped forward.

Reece cleared his throat.

Flushing, I looked away from the unnerving intensity in Colton's gaze. A shiver chased after his hand as it slipped off the back of my neck and dropped to his side.

"I need you to tell me exactly what happened at the store," Colton said after a moment, his voice rougher than normal.

I did exactly that.

It was odd to have both Colton and Reece in my bedroom. Their presence made it feel much smaller than it was. Any other time I would've been amused by having two extraordinarily attractive brothers who were also cops standing in front of me, but I was too thrown by everything.

The murder last night.

Colton showing up this morning with crepes.

Creepy van dude.

Vandalized property.

And now the way Colton behaved when he showed up and that...that spark? My skin was still tingling.

All within twenty-four hours. It was insane. My life was normally boring.

By the time I answered all of Colton's questions, it was just us in the house. Reece had left not too long after the other officer to answer another call, and it was close to ten.

Colton had gone downstairs to make a few calls and I was slow to follow him. A warm breeze stirred the curtains in front of the broken window and my gaze drifted to the floor. The glass was gone. The TV was also righted, its broken face a sad sight.

Stepping off the stairs, I looked into the kitchen just in time to see Colton dumping the glass in the trash can. He was still on the phone.

"That's what I thought," I heard him say as he placed the dustpan on the counter. "You know how he operates. We all know how he works." There was a pause as he turned around. His eyes met mine. "Yeah," he spoke into the phone. "I'll be in touch."

Suddenly self-conscious, I glanced at the window and then back at him as I stood near the stairwell. "Thank you for cleaning up. You didn't have to do that."

He placed his phone on the counter and started toward me. Goose bumps raced across my flesh. "Do you have something to cover the window with tonight? Tomorrow I can head down to the hardware store and get some boards to cover it until someone can get out here and replace it."

Did I fall and hit my head? "You don't have to do that. Thank you, but—"

"I know I don't have to do it. I want to do it." With his long-legged pace, it took him no time to end up standing in front of me. "I'm off tomorrow, and I have time now unless I get a call."

I tilted my head back to meet his stare as I weighed whether I should accept his help. It seemed stupid not to, but it was a lot for him to do for...for me. "I don't want you to go out of your way, Colton."

One side of his lips kicked up. "I don't mind going out of my way for you." He put his hand on the stairway railing above me. "Not at all."

The crazed, possibly carnivorous, butterfly flutter from this morning was back, wiggling around in my stomach.

"Let me help you with this," he urged softly.

I drew in a shallow breath. "Okay."

The smile grew as he lifted his hand from the railing and caught a piece of my hair, brushing it back from my cheek. "Now that wasn't so hard, was it?"

It was and I didn't even understand why.

"Do you have a tarp that I could use to cover the window?" he asked.

"There is one in the shed out back. It was there when I moved in and I don't know if it's any good or not."

"I'll check it out." He started to turn and then stopped. Placing the tips of his fingers under my chin, he tilted my head back. There was a good chance my heart stopped. "Can I ask you something?"

At that moment, he could probably do anything he wanted. "Sure."

The dimple appeared on his left cheek and then he bit down on his lower lip. Something about that tugged at the very core of me. I wanted to be his teeth. Or his lip. Hell, I'd be down for any part of that.

"Do you believe in second chances?" he asked.

That was not the question I was expecting him to ask, but my answer was immediate and it was the truth, something I felt deeply. "Yes."

"Good." His finger slipped up my chin and his thumb smoothed along the skin under my lip. "So do I."

Chapter 7

Luck was finally shining down on me. The tarp Colton gathered from the shed was useable. I put on a pot of coffee while he broke out the duct tape, and then I pretended not to be watching him cover my window.

I was totally watching him. I mean, who wouldn't? When he'd spread out the tarp, he'd bent over and good Lord in sweet, sweet heaven, that man had a *great* rear end. And then when he started hanging it up, I was witness to the amazing display of muscles rippling and straining under his shirt.

What I would give to see that man in the buff.

During this, I did make a mental note to contact my insurance company on Monday morning, so I wasn't a complete fail at prioritizing.

I walked his cup over to him, placing it on the coffee table. Working on one corner, he glanced over his shoulder. "Thanks."

Since I had tried to help already and was virtually shooed away, I sat on the couch. "I really do appreciate this."

"It's no problem." He ripped off the section of the tape. "There're a couple of things I need to talk to you about. I was planning on filling you in tomorrow. Maybe over some pancakes this time."

I squeezed my eyes shut briefly and wished his words meant more than just charming flirtatiousness. "Okay."

"We've identified the victim." He stretched the tarp down the right side as he filled me in. "Not the most upstanding citizen, but his record was mostly petty crimes, a few drug infractions. Looks like what went down Friday night might have been more of a turf thing, but obviously it's bigger than that."

My spine stiffened. "I figured as much. Creepy van dude gave me that impression."

"The man murdered worked for Isaiah Vakhrov. Have you ever heard of him?"

"No. Should I have?"

He shook his head as he tore off another piece of tape. "Not if you want to live a long, healthy and safe life, no. Isaiah Vakhrov pretty much runs the city, but not from the right side of the fence, if you get what I'm saying. His fingers are in everything. Some of his business is legit and some of it's not. Lot of drugs come in and out of this city because of him."

I frowned. "So, he's some kind of crime lord? And everyone knows this? How is he still doing what he does?"

"Cause like I said, he's got his hands in a lot of things, and that means he's got a lot of people in his pocket. He's Teflon. Nothing sticks."

"Wow," I murmured.

"Anyway, the man murdered worked for Isaiah, and one thing every shitbag in this state and the ones touching ours knows is you don't mess with Isaiah's people unless you want a target on the back of your head. Whoever the shooters are, either aren't the brightest or they have more balls than brains. And whoever they work for doesn't want that connection made," he told me. "Which explains what happened at the store and this. Someone ID'd you. Could've been anyone hanging around the crime scene Friday night or…"

Or it could've been someone in the police department. Good God, this was unreal.

"The thing is, knowing Isaiah, he's going to find out who pulled that trigger before us." His laugh was without humor. "He almost always does. And he's going to take care of it. But what I don't like is whoever the punks work for coming after you." He yanked on the tape. "They're not going to get close to you again."

The way he said it almost had me convinced he could single-handedly ensure that. I wanted to believe that, but he couldn't be around me twenty-four hours a day. The fear I'd been holding back pressed on me. "Should I...should I be worried about this Isaiah?"

"Honestly?" The muscles moved along his spine. "No. But he's not a good guy. Don't ever mistake him for that, but he has his own sense of moral code and conduct. Violence against women or children is a surefire way to get on his bad side. He will leave you alone."

"That's sort of comforting," I mumbled, taking a sip of my coffee. "Kind of."

"Gotta say, though, you're handling all of this like a champ."

I got a wee bit distracted by the way his bicep bunched and blurted out, "I cried myself to sleep last night."

Colton stilled.

My eyes widened. "Oh my God." I placed my hand over my forehead. "I cannot believe I just said that out loud."

Lowering his hands, he let the tarp flap to the side as he faced me. The roll of duct tape dangled from his fingers.

Warmth invaded my cheeks. "I mean, I didn't like sob or anything, and I don't cry a lot. It's just that—"

"Honey, you don't have to explain anything. You saw some shit last night." Dropping the roll of tape on the arm of the chair, he walked around the coffee table and got right in between it and me. Plucking the cup out of my hand, he placed it beside his and sat on the corner of the table in front of me. He was so close our knees pressed together when he leaned in, resting his arms on his thighs. "Having an emotional reaction is expected. If you hadn't, I would be concerned. To be honest, I didn't like the idea of you being alone after seeing something like that."

"Why?" I asked before I could stop myself. "Why do you care?"

He tilted his head to the side. "I'm not sure what to think about that kind of question."

I exhaled slowly. "I mean, do you treat all your witnesses this way? Bring them crepes in the morning and fix vandalized windows?"

Colton raised a brow. "No."

Well, that was a blunt answer. "Then why are you doing it now?"

"When I asked you if you believed in second chances, I was hoping you'd say yes." Those thick lashes lifted. "I don't like the way our paths crossed again, but I'm glad they did."

There were no words.

A playful grin appeared. "I noticed you in high school, Abby. I thought you were pretty and smart. I liked how you were always the first one in the class and the last one out."

Oh my God, I was always the first one in and the last one out.

"I liked how you were nice to everyone, even the assholes who didn't deserve it," he continued, those azure eyes glimmering. "So, yeah, I noticed you, but you had a boyfriend. You always had a boyfriend. I respected that, but I know you noticed me."

The warmth increasing in my cheeks had nothing to do with embarrassment.

"You know, every couple of years, you've crossed my mind. That's the damn truth." His eyes met mine and held. "It was always unexpected. Never unwelcomed. Did you think of me?"

"Yes. I've thought of you," I whispered.

His grin turned smug. "Hell yeah."

Stunned by what he was admitting, it still didn't make sense. "I've seen you around town, Colton, since I moved back. At the store or the movies." I left out the part that he was with someone else because that was irrelevant. "You never noticed me then."

"Then I'm a fucking idiot if that's true."

I blinked and my gaze centered on his well-formed mouth. What did his mouth feel like? Was it hard? Soft? A mixture of both? And what did he taste like? I bet a marvelous mix of coffee and man. "Colton—"

"I should've noticed you. Damn, I hate the idea that I hadn't." Sincerity filled his tone. "I notice you now, Abby."

My heart started tripping all over itself. "This doesn't seem real."

A chuckle rumbled out of him. "Why not?"

"Because these things don't happen in real life," I told him, leaning back and needing the space before I decided to find out exactly how his mouth felt and what he tasted like. "They don't."

His brows knitted together. "This is happening. It's real life."

"You are not getting what I'm saying." I drew in a deep breath. "Extremely gorgeous men like you—"

"You think I'm extremely gorgeous?" His grin reappeared and so did the left dimple.

I shot him a bland look. "Like you don't know that. And see, that's the thing. You're the gorgeous, confident cop and I'm not the worst thing walking on two legs, but I'm not the type of woman who snags the interest of a guy like you. That only happens in books."

He stared at me for a moment and then he shook his head. "First off, what the hell do you mean by woman like you?"

"Do I really need to spell it out for you?"

His eyes narrowed. "Yeah, yeah you do."

Frustration rose, racing across my skin like an army of fire ants. He couldn't be serious. "I don't look like the woman I saw you at the movies with. She was a tall, thin *beautiful* blonde. No one in this world would describe me as *that* beautiful woman with the hot guy. They would be like, wow, he's really with someone quite average. And I'm totally okay with being that average chick. I know what I am, so this doesn't make sense. I mean, unless you're just horny and want to get laid and you have no other prospects at the moment, then that makes more sense, I guess."

He opened his mouth, closed it, and then tried again. "If I'm horny and want to get laid?"

Yeah, I sort of couldn't believe I said that myself.

"Honey, how old do you think I am that all I'm about is getting laid?" he asked.

"Well, I mean, I get horny and want to get laid too, and we're roughly the same age." I really needed to shut up. "All I'm trying to say is that it's human nature."

"Human nature?" His blue eyes brightened as he laughed under his breath. "Can I just tell you that I'm thrilled to hear you get horny, and honey, you want to get laid, I'm your man, but you don't really know me, Abby."

I was still stuck on him being my man if I wanted to get laid, and boy, did I ever want to get laid. Hadn't even really considered it seriously in the last four years. No guy had sparked my attention, but right now? An ache had already blossomed and my breath came in and out in little shallow bursts, a reaction just to the mere idea of sleeping with him.

"And we're going to change that," Colton said. "You and I are going to get to know each other in a way that's long overdue."

My breath caught as a tight shiver coiled. "We are?"

That half grin did crazy-insane things to me. "Oh, we are. You know why? Because we got a second chance to do so and we aren't going to miss that, are we?"

I couldn't look away. "No?"

"That's right." Lifting his arm, he cupped my cheek with his hand. "Here's an important piece of information about me. If I'm looking for just a lay, I'm not going to bring that woman crepes in the morning or fix her window. And I'm sure as hell not going to risk my career to just screw around with a witness. If I'm going to take that risk, it's going to be worth it." His thumb dragged under my lip, causing me to suck in a shallow breath. "And honey, I have a good feeling, you're worth it."

Before I could respond, before I could say anything that would probably ruin everything he'd just said, he slipped that hand along my cheek, his fingers tangling in my hair as he leaned in, forcing his knee between mine. I took a breath. My heart beat. All I saw was the blue of his eyes.

And then Colton kissed me.

Chapter 8

Every enjoyable, exaggerated thing my authors have ever written about being kissed was totally true, and it had been so long since I'd been kissed that I'd forgotten that.

The moment his lips touched mine, my body flushed hot, and it was a gentle kiss, nothing more than a light sweeping of his lips across mine—once and then twice. As if he were slowly mapping out the feel of my lips, he took his time familiarizing himself.

And then he caught my lower lip between his, creating a mad flutter in my stomach. The hand on my cheek shifted and his long fingers cradled the back of my head as he lifted his mouth from mine. His eyes burned a blue fire. There was a questioning in his gaze, and when I didn't pull away, his hand tightened.

Colton kissed me again, full on, and his lips *were* an amazing combination of soft and hard, satin stretched over steel.

My hand fell to his chest and the other to his knee as I felt the tip of his tongue tracing the seam of my mouth. My lips parted, and that kiss deepened. I tasted the coffee on his tongue and I knew he tasted me.

At first, I didn't really move. I let him lead the way, take that kiss in a direction that caused my blood to simmer, but when his tongue touched mine, it was like I woke up. My senses came alive. Every nerve ending in my body fired all at once.

This...*this* was what I had been missing.

Tilting my head to the side, I slipped my hand around his neck, anchoring his mouth to mine. I kissed him back, devouring *him*.

"Fuck," he groaned, and then he was moving.

Not away, but standing, and then he was hovering over me, his other hand curving around my hip. He lifted me, and I wasn't a small girl. I marveled in the act as he laid me on my back, his mouth never leaving mine. One elbow planted into the cushion of the couch beside my head, and he kept his body off mine even as the demand of his lips increased and the pleasure of his mouth moving over mine heightened.

I didn't know a kiss could feel like this.

Like he was touching every part of me.

I clung to him, willing him to lower his body to mine so that I could feel his weight. A shiver worked its way across my skin as my fingers sifted through the soft brush of hair along the nape of his neck. He tasted decadent, a deep, rich maleness.

And when he lifted his mouth again, I whimpered from the loss. Actually, *whimpered*. "I like that sound," he said in a rich, sensual voice. "Really fucking like it."

Colton kissed me once more. "There're a few things I want to get straight."

"Does that require talking?"

His answering chuckle brushed my lips. "It does." There was a pause as his mouth brushed the corner of my lips. "But I can multitask."

"Thank God," I whispered.

His body shook with another laugh and then his mouth was moving along the curve of my jaw. "You're not pretty."

My eyes flew open and widened. "Excuse me?"

"I don't think you're pretty." His mouth found my pulse. "I think you're fucking beautiful."

"Oh." I gasped as my hand curled around the straining bicep. A warmth grew in my chest.

"I thought you were beautiful damn near a decade ago." The hot, wet lick against my pulse caused my back to arch. "With your dark hair and fair skin, you were like a living Snow White." That mouth of his was on the move, coasting down my throat, scattering my thoughts. "I don't have a type, Abby. I don't go for just blondes or whatever." With his other hand, he worked my shirt to the side, baring my shoulder. "Checkered?"

At first, I didn't get what he was referencing, but then I felt his finger trailing the lacy strap of my bra. "I think checkered print is underrated."

He laughed and then he pressed a kiss to the hollow of my throat. "And something else I want you to understand, Abby. You're not average. You could never be average."

My breath caught. "You barely know me."

Blazing a trail of fiery little kisses across my collarbone, he dragged his hand down my side, over my waist, to the flare of my hip once more. "Nothing about you screams average. Never did. I know damn well that hasn't changed."

This had to be a dream.

His hand squeezed my hip as he coasted those lips all the way back to mine, kissing me slowly, deeply. Blue fire still burned in his eyes when his gaze met mine.

Then he slowly pressed down, the hardest part of him against the softest part of me. I gasped at the feel of the heavy bulge. Liquid heat pooled. A tempting warmth built inside of me, a raw fire. God, I hadn't felt this way in...

"That's what you do to me," he said, nipping at my lip as he rocked his hips against mine. Desire darted through my veins. Goodness, he was—there were no words. "You get what I'm showing you?" he asked, lust hardening his words.

Part of me did. There was the other part that couldn't comprehend his interest, and finally, another part that wanted to stop talking and start kissing again.

But that second part of me won out. "Where do you see this going?"

He didn't answer immediately, and in that short space, reality kicked in. Maybe this wasn't the best time to ask that question, but what were we doing? Last night had been the first time we'd talked in years and now we were kissing? Hell, we were doing more than kissing. I was flat on my back and he knew I was wearing a checkered print bra.

And I also now knew that all areas of his body were exceptionally well-proportioned; something in my wildest dreams I never thought I'd ever have personal knowledge of.

I thoroughly believed in insta-lust. Criminy, I'd experienced it several times at the gym, but I was never one to act on it. Or was I? I never really had the chance to do so. I'd never given myself the chance.

But this seemed so fast, because it was fast. Possibly record-breaking fast, but he, the guy I'd admired from afar for quite some time, thought I was beautiful. And he thought there wasn't a single thing about me that screamed *average*.

My wry gaze flicked over his handsome face as the seconds ticked by. Uncertainty slammed into me. "Colton, I—"

His mouth silenced my words, but the softness of his kiss, the tenderness behind it, quelled the brimming disquiet. When he spoke, his nose grazed mine. "That's a hard question to answer, but you know what I do know, Abby? Despite how you came back into my life last night, I was thrilled to see you. I came over this morning because I wanted to see you again and I didn't want to wait for a better excuse. I'm impatient like that," he added, and I felt his lips form a grin against mine. "And I kissed you and I am right where I am because I want you. I think you can feel that."

"I can feel that," I said, my voice throaty. There was no way I couldn't feel that.

"And I think the way you kissed me back tells me you are right where you are because you want to be here." He kissed me softly, stirring up the flutter into a crazy spiral. He lifted his head slightly and stared down at me. "I don't know where this is going or what to expect, but I know what I want and I'm the type of guy that goes for it. Why would I wait getting that message across? It doesn't feel like something that's going to change in a week or a month."

The type of guy who goes for it.

Was it really that simple? He wanted me, so he was going to go for it. Why waste the time? Could it really be that simple for me? Because I did want him. I wanted him so badly it was a physical ache. And why did I really need to even think about the future, where this could lead? We were both consenting adults, and there was no mistaking the fact that he was attracted to me. Could I pass this up?

Pass up the chance to feel again? To be alive?

Because that would be what I was doing if I listened to the tiny, annoying voices in the back of my head. In the hours spent here and there with Colton, I'd felt more than I had in the four years since Kevin passed on. The most I felt was through the words and stories I edited. Was there something wrong with wanting to feel alive again, for wanting more?

I hoped not.

"Okay," I whispered, placing my shaking hand on his cheek, drawing his mouth back toward mine.

Colton came willingly, and his breath hitched before he closed his mouth over mine. There was nothing sweet about this kiss. Our lips parted, and his tongue was a hot, moist demand inside my mouth. He took complete control, as if he was staking his claim, and there was a possessiveness in the way he kissed that shattered memories of any other kiss.

He splayed his palm flat against my cheek, still for a moment, and then he glided it down my neck. His hand stayed there, the touch gentle and so at odds with the fierceness of the kiss. I moaned, my body arching toward his, wanting to melt into him. Between my thighs, I pulsed and I ached. I was so into the taste and feel of him, but that voice was in the back of my head, this time preaching a different story.

Could I actually get naked in front of him?

Speaking of getting naked, I was pretty sure the Hanes boy shorts I was wearing were the least possible sexy thing I could have on, along with the checkered bra.

Would he still be so aroused once he realized there was more cushion for the pushin'?

His pelvis thrust against mine, scattering those fears like ashes in the wind. He nipped at my lower lip, the tiny bite sending a wave of pleasure through my veins.

Making a deep sound in the back of his throat, he lifted his mouth from mine. "I really need to fix that window."

"What window?" I murmured, dazed.

Colton laughed as he dipped his head into the space between my neck and shoulder. "Cute."

"What?"

"You're cute." He kissed my neck. "You can be cute."

I opened my eyes. "I thought I was beautiful?"

"You're both." Pushing himself up, he paused just long enough to kiss me again and then he popped up onto his feet with grace I was envious of. "It's good to be both."

"Uh-huh." I was still lying there, half sprawled on the couch, trying to get control of my thoughts and breathing. I wetted my lips that felt swollen.

Colton extended a hand. "If you stay like that, I'm going to be way too tempted."

I glanced up at him. "What's wrong with being tempted?"

His lips parted. "Damn if I remember right now."

That brought a smile to my face. Placing my hand in his, I let him pull me up into a sitting position. "The window," I reminded him.

"Oh yeah, that. Guess we need to get that fixed so we aren't giving your neighbors a show."

My eyes widened. Holy crapola, I hadn't even thought of that.

Colton started to turn away, but stopped. A soft smile played across his lips. "You know something? It's been a long time since I started a day and ended it with a woman. Glad it's you."

Chapter 9

Sunday morning, I did something I hadn't done in a very long time. When I stripped off my pajamas and shoved the shower door open, I didn't allow myself to gloss over my reflection or to pretend that I wasn't purposely avoiding catching a glimpse of myself. Because that was what I'd been doing for a long time. Almost like if I didn't see myself, I didn't have to acknowledge how I felt.

But this morning, I looked.

The hollows of my cheeks were a bright pink and my gaze wary as I took in my disheveled hair. It was probably my imagination, but my lips looked swollen. There was no way that was the case, but I didn't have to try hard to remember Colton's kisses. My lips tingled. Those kisses were something I wouldn't forget.

My gaze drifted down, over the slope of my shoulders and then across my chest. I pressed my lips together as I lifted my hands, placing them over my breasts. The skin was smooth, nipples puckered. Steam began to fill the bathroom, dampening my skin. I lowered my hands. My breasts were round and full. Definitely nowhere in the general vicinity of perkiness, but they...they matched the rest of me. My waist curved in slightly and then flared out, forming round hips. The shadowy area between my plump thighs drew my attention. Brazilian wax? Uh, no. I almost laughed out loud at that thought.

God, it had been so long since I had sex.

Could I do it? An image of Colton formed in my thoughts, and the flush raced down my throat. Biting down on my lip, I was pretty sure that I could do it. The man neared perfection when it came to his body.

That would be a lot to overcome.

As I twisted to the side, peeking at my behind, I tried to come to terms with how I felt about myself. It wasn't easy and the steam covered the mirror before I had any answer. I stepped into the shower, letting the hot water beat down on me. I wasn't sure if it was a lack of self-esteem or a lack of action that had my confidence bouncing all over the place. Or maybe it was the fact that I spent every day caught up in the fictional worlds of the authors I edited, experienced their love, their heartbreak and everything in between that I hadn't, in the last four years, experienced anything in the real world or taken any time for myself.

When Kevin passed away, I had thrown myself into work. If I was honest, that was when I started to lose sight of myself, of who I was. I didn't want that any longer. Last night I had decided that I couldn't pass up the chance to feel again. And what I saw in the mirror wasn't horrifying. It was the same body Kevin used to refer to as Botticelli beautiful. Curves weren't a bad thing.

I just needed to get my mind on board with all of that.

Since I had gotten up early, I hit the computer after I'd showered and changed into a pair of jeans and a loose, cap sleeve blouse. I was able to work on a couple of pages before my phone dinged. It was a text from Colton. He was outside.

Heart jumping all around like a bouncing bean, I saved my work and closed the laptop. My bare feet were silent as I came down the stairs. The fresh pot of coffee I'd put on scented the air. Reaching the door, I opened it with a deep breath.

And the same breath punched out of my lungs.

The jeans he wore were faded along the knee and the old screen T-shirt stretched across his broad shoulders. He lived in these kinds of clothes. Not dress shirts and pants, and while he looked good in his detective getup, he looked *damn* good in jeans.

"Mornin'," Colton drawled, stepping inside. He held a white cardboard box that smelled like heaven, and as I moved to close the door, he swooped down, pressing his lips against my cheek. The innocent brush of his lips across my skin sent an acute shiver down my spine. "I swung by the hardware store and picked up the stuff."

Closing the door, I ordered myself to pull it together. "And the bakery?"

"Always the bakery." He tossed a grin over his shoulder as he headed toward the kitchen, where he placed the box on the counter. "I got some muffins and éclairs. You haven't eaten yet, right?"

My tummy grumbled happily. "No. Thank you for doing that—for doing all of this."

"Like I said before, my pleasure. Do you prefer chocolate or fruit?"

I watched him from under my lashes. "Chocolate. Always chocolate."

He chuckled as he plucked the chocolate éclair out, placing it on a napkin. "I'll have to remember that." Picking up a fruity éclair, he faced me and leaned back against the counter. "Did you sleep well last night?"

At first, I had tossed and turned, thinking about his kiss and what he'd said. I'd been turned on and I had to take care of that. Not that I was going to share that piece of info. Obviously. "I slept okay. You?"

His lashes lowered as a small grin tugged at his lips. "It took me a while to fall asleep."

Could he have had the same problem as I? An image of him took hold in my thoughts, vibrant and seductive. I saw him in bed, his hand beneath the sheet, gripping his cock. My stomach hollowed at the thought, my mouth dried. His back would definitely be bowing and his head would be kicked back against the pillows as he worked himself…

He tilted his head to the side. "What are you thinking about, Abby?"

"Nothing." Turning away hastily, I all but shoved the éclair in my mouth. "So…um, how much do I owe you for the stuff to fix the window?"

"Dinner."

I dabbed at my lips when I turned back around. My brows rose. "Dinner?"

A half grin appeared. "Yes. Dinner. You know, where two people, sometimes more, go out to eat?" He took a bite of his éclair while my eyes narrowed. "Tonight."

I started to ask why but managed to stop myself before I looked like a complete idiot. Well, I wasn't sure I would look like a moron, but it would be so evident that my confidence in what was going on between us was somewhere between crappy and craptastic.

So I smiled as excitement and hope bubbled, and prayed there wasn't chocolate on my teeth. "Dinner would be nice."

* * * *

Colton was as handy as he was good looking, and I really could get used to him doing work around the house. Actually, I could get used to him just being in my house in general.

As he boarded up the window, making it more secure until the window guys could come out, an easy conversation flowed back and forth between us, and it was the same when he reappeared later that evening to take me to dinner.

After he'd left in the late afternoon, the struggle had been real when it came to concentrating, but I managed to get some work done on McGuire's novel. I was lucky; her manuscripts were typically clean.

Nervous giddiness had my heart and pulse jumping all around as I picked out a dress that I hadn't worn in what felt like forever. Actually, there was a good chance I'd never worn the sleeveless pink and blue floral dress. I sort of felt like I was wearing my grandmother's couch when I slipped it on over my head, but the high waist and heart-shaped neckline were super flattering. I felt pretty in the dress.

Maybe even a little sexy.

I carried a pair of pink heels downstairs and then slipped them on mere moments before there was a knock on my door. Colton had texted, letting me know he was there. With my heart lodged somewhere in my throat, I opened the door and my tongue nearly lolled out of my mouth and rolled across the floor.

Once again dressed in jeans, he'd paired the dark denim with a plain, white button-down shirt with the sleeves rolled up to his elbows, showcasing powerful forearms. I didn't know what it was about sleeves rolled up, but it had always been a huge turn-on for me.

I was so weird.

Colton's gaze glided over me as a small grin appeared. "You look lovely."

Like I was love-struck or something equally silly, I felt my cheeks flush. "Thank you. So do you. I mean, you don't look lovely. You look hot. Sexy. Very nice."

His brows rose.

I wanted to smack myself. "I think I'll stop talking now."

He chuckled as he lowered his head, kissing me softly. "Actually, keep talking. It's doing wonders for my ego."

"I don't think you need any help in that department."

"True," he admitted, straightening. "My head is probably already too big."

The thing was, Colton was confident and self-assured, maybe even a little cocky, but he wasn't arrogant. He was like a unicorn.

"You ready?"

"Just one second." I grabbed my purse and keys off the coffee table and then joined him outside, pulling the door closed behind me. The heat was near stifling, coating my skin as I glanced at the boarded window. I cringed. "That looks terrible."

"Not the greatest curb appeal," he agreed, placing his hand on my lower back. We started down the short set of steps. "Did you get in touch with anyone today after I left?"

"I called my insurance company—the one-eight-hundred number. It doesn't make sense to file a claim, not with the deductible, but they did give me a list of companies to call tomorrow." Despite the heat, I couldn't suppress a shiver when he slid his hand to the center of my back.

He cast me a knowing side-look as we stepped onto the sidewalk. "I want someone to get out here quick. I don't like the idea of the window being like that for long."

"Me neither. I feel like—"

A loud pop caused me to jump and lose my grip on my purse. It slipped from my fingers, falling to the pavement as I whipped around. Heart racing, my frantic gaze searched for the source of the sound, terrified I was about to come face-to-face with the bald man.

He wasn't there.

"Are you okay?" Colton placed his hand on my shoulder, turning me toward him. Concern was etched into his handsome face. "Abby?"

"Was that a...a gun?" The moment I spoke the question, I already knew the answer. If it had been a gun, I doubted Colton would just be standing there. "I'm sorry." My cheeks burned as I looked away. "I know that wasn't what that was."

"It was a car backfiring. Probably down the street." His hand curved around the nape of my neck and he guided my gaze back to his. "I get it."

That was all he needed to say and I believed him. Nodding slowly, I forced an even breath in and then out. "I guess…I'm just a little jumpy after Friday. When I heard that, I thought…"

"I'm not surprised." His hand shifted and he curled his arm around my shoulders, drawing me to his chest. "You freaking amaze me, Abby, with how you're holding it together after Friday, but I know it has effected you and that's okay. That's normal."

The citrusy scent of his cologne surrounded me and my heart rate slowed. The embarrassment from overreacting eased off. "Thank you."

"There is no reason you need to thank me." Leaning back, he brushed his lips over my forehead and then lowered his arm. He swooped down, picking up my purse. "But I want you to feel safe. Nothing is going to happen to you."

I didn't respond as he took my hand in his other one. Still holding my purse, he led me to where his truck was parked under a large oak tree. The leaves stirred in the warm breeze. "Reece has been keeping an eye on your place during the night and throughout the day, doing drive-bys."

I stared at him, floored.

"It's not perfect, but I doubt you're ready for me camping out in your place like I want to until we get those shitheads and put them behind bars." Stopping in front of the passenger door, he let go of my hand and opened it. "Up?"

I didn't move, not even when he placed the purse in my hands. "You have Reece watching my place?"

"Yeah. And the other deputies know to keep an eye out." He cocked his head to the side, studying me. "You look like I just dropped my pants."

I liked to think I'd be rocking a totally different look on my face if he'd done that. "I'm just surprised. That's a lot of trouble for them."

"It's nothing." His gaze met mine. "And they're glad to do it. You're important to me. They know that."

For the umpteenth time since he appeared Friday night, I was absolutely flummoxed by Colton. I was important to him? Since when? That question sounded like such a douche-tastic thing to think, but could he really be telling the truth? Did I have any reason to doubt that he was?

"You have that look on your face," he said.

I snapped out of it. "What look?"

"Like you don't believe a word I'm saying."

My eyes widened. Was I that obvious? Holy crap. But he didn't get it. He didn't understand that there was a part of me, no matter how much attention or attraction he tossed in my direction or what he said, that couldn't truly believe he really wanted all of this with me.

"That's okay." He tapped my hip with his hand, motioning me to get into the truck. I did just that, staring at him as he closed the door and jogged around the front. When he climbed in, he started the truck, cranking up the air conditioner. Snagging aviator-style sunglasses off the visor, he slipped them on and looked over at me. "Do you know why it's okay?"

I shook my head. "I'm guessing you're going to tell me?"

His lips kicked up on one corner. "Nah, sweetheart, I'm going to show you."

* * * *

I'm going to show you.

Those words lingered in the back of my head throughout dinner, a tantalizing distraction that resurfaced whenever our gazes collided. Conversation wasn't lacking though.

While we waited for the food to arrive, along with the wine, we chatted about high school and he asked about college. I talked about what it was like to live in a city like New York, and he'd admitted that he could never handle day in and day out in the city, not even Philadelphia. During the dinner, he led me into a conversation about editing, something that many people outside of the publishing industry would have absolutely no interest in, but he seemed genuinely curious about it.

And when I started to go fan-girl over the authors I worked with and hoped to work with in the future, he said I was cute. Again.

We didn't talk about the investigation. I hadn't brought it up, figuring it would kind of ruin the lovely dinner.

Sometimes I found myself missing what he was saying, just tiny bits, because as terrible as it sounded, I ended up just staring at him. It wasn't just because he was that attractive. It was more than a physical thing. A mixture of his charm and kindness, the fact that he was actually here, after all this time, having dinner with me, had a lot to do with it. And yeah, some of it had to do with him simply being so freaking hot.

And I was woman enough to admit that.

I had to wonder what people thought when they saw us together. Like when the waitress's gaze lingered on Colton, what crossed her mind? Did she wonder how the hell I ended up on a date with someone like Colton, who was universally attractive? No one wanted to admit it, but I knew people thought things like that. Hell, I had. After all, if they didn't, there wouldn't be a thousand articles online showcasing couples that didn't match on the attractive scale.

Maybe I wasn't giving myself enough credit. I didn't want to think about things like that right now, because the dinner was sort of perfect, and the steady internal stream of nonsense was ruining it.

Night had fallen when we left the restaurant and bright stars blanketed the onyx sky. He kept his hand on my lower back until we reached his truck. It was such a simple gesture, but I felt like there was so much meaning to it.

The ride back to my place was quiet as I was lost in my own thoughts, replaying the dinner over and over. I wasn't even aware of the fact that we were at my house until he parked the truck.

I glanced at him in the dark interior of the truck, half hopeful that he would come in and partly terrified that he would.

One hand rested on the steering wheel as his gaze met mine and held. His features were shadowed, so I had no idea what he was thinking. "Walk you to the door?"

"Sure." Disappointment snapped at my heels. So he didn't want to come in? Did I want him to come in? Colton dropped his hand from the steering wheel and reached over, and as he unbuckled my seatbelt, his hand brushed along my stomach. A series of shivers danced over my skin.

Oh yeah, I wanted him to come in. Like that door was wide open.

We walked to the front door, silent with the exception of the humming of crickets. I didn't know what to say when we reached my door and I dug my keys out, unlocking it. I wished I could be brave and confident, invite him in with a sexy little grin, but it had been so long since I'd done this.

Actually, I'd never really done this before. Kevin and I had done the dating thing while in high school. Parents were involved then. Dates ended at the door and picked up again with late-night phone calls. This was a whole different ballpark I had no experience in. I looked up at him, drawing in a shallow breath.

He was staring down at me, and even though I couldn't see his eyes, I could *feel* his gaze, it was that intense. "I had a really good time tonight."

"So did I." I was breathless as I opened the door and stepped inside. When I turned to him and looked up once more, whatever I was about to say faded, lost in the space between us.

There was a certain intent to the line of his mouth, and I knew before he even lowered his head, that he was going to kiss me. The breath I took got stuck in my throat as he cupped my cheek with one hand, tilting my head back. He brushed his lips over mine like he had done the night before, tentative and questioning. There was something so sweet about the kiss as we stood with me just inside the door and him leaning in.

Last night had been the first time I'd been kissed in four years. This being the second time, instinct quickly took over. Or maybe it was simply just arousal. Pleasure darted as I tilted my head to the side, and when the tip of his tongue touched the seam of my mouth, sweetness was the furthest thing from my mind.

The kiss deepened as our tongues tangled. My hands ended up on his chest and his delved into my hair as his arm circled my waist, drawing me tight to his front. I felt him then, hard against my belly, and feeling just how effected he was had my blood simmering.

The fear of things escalating took a backseat, still there but not consuming my attention. I couldn't think around his kisses, could barely breathe, and somehow, we were moving. I heard the door slam shut behind us and then my back was pressed against the wall and there was no space between us.

"I've been wanting to do that since I saw you in this dress," he admitted, and then kissed me before I could respond.

I clung to his shoulders as his hand slipped down my side, curling around my thigh, just below my hip, leaving behind a wake of shivers.

Lifting his mouth from mine, he breathed heavily. "I told myself I was going to behave tonight."

My hands clenched over his shoulders, wrinkling the material of his shirt. "You're not?"

He kissed my jaw. "Well, I was planning on being a gentleman."

"Why?" I asked, surprising myself.

"Hell. Good question." His lips moved over my neck as I tipped my head back against the wall. "I'm not even sure."

I gasped when I felt his tongue circle where my pulse pounded.

"I just can't keep my hands off you." He lifted my leg just enough that he was able to settle his hips against my core, and oh God, the ache that blossomed almost made me weep. "Damn," he groaned, burying his face in my neck. "That didn't help."

My chest rose and fell sharply. "No. No, it didn't."

A deep groan rumbled out of him, and I felt his hand on my thigh move, slipping under the hem of my skirt. The glide of his palm against my bare skin shook me, pushing a soft moan out from between my parted lips, and that was nothing compared to what came next. He dragged his hand up and over, cupping my rear as he pushed his hips in. Muscles coiled in response.

He dragged his lips up my throat, finding my mouth as his hand kneaded my bottom. The kiss rocked me, and there was little doubt in my mind that I'd stop him if he pulled my panties down and took me right against the wall. The mere thought of him doing so burned my skin, twisted up my insides in a crazy way.

The attraction I felt toward him was startling.

His kiss slowed as he dragged his hand out from under my dress. "Okay," he murmured. "I told myself I wasn't going to do this tonight."

I opened my eyes, barely making out his features in the soft glow radiating from the stairwell light. My heart thundered. I wanted to tell him to ignore what he'd told himself. I was damp between the thighs, ready and wanting. I *wanted* him.

Colton lowered my leg as he rested his forehead against mine. His chest rose just as rapidly. I didn't say anything as we both struggled to gain control over what our bodies demanded, but him putting the brakes on where this was heading was obviously the smart thing to do.

All of this felt so fast and I knew it could quickly get out of hand, but I…I wanted it to do that. I liked Colton. I'd liked him in high school. I'd liked him from afar when I'd moved back home. I really, *really* liked him now.

And that was terrifying.

Chapter 10

Hitting *send* on the e-mail, I smiled at the computer screen. I'd busted ass since I'd woken up, foregoing showering and even changing out of pajamas until I reached the last page.

The glamorous life of an editor.

Finished with the edits, I pushed out of my chair and picked up a dry erase pen. Carrying it to the whiteboard hung near the desk, I scratched a line over *Other Lives*. Nothing made me more giddy than marking something off from my to-do list.

Actually, that wasn't entirely true.

Colton took the top spot of things that made me giddy right about now.

This last week had been...absolutely amazing, almost like I was a teen again or in my early twenties, buzzing around happily. I'd forgotten how it feels, to be...to be caught up in the excitement and anticipation of seeing someone, to actually be feeling something strongly again, because if this week had taught me anything, it was that the last four years had been only about my career and nothing else.

But this week had also taught me a lot more.

Since Colton worked ten-hour shifts, he had three days off—Sunday, Monday, and oddly, Wednesday. Of course, he was on call those days and it didn't seem like he really had them off. Due to the shooting last week, he was in the office both Monday and Wednesday, following up on leads, but both evenings I spent time with him. Monday was the movies, something I hadn't really enjoyed since Kevin. Wednesday we grabbed dinner at this restaurant in town, one I'd never been to before because it seemed like a couples kind of place.

Both nights had ended like Sunday night, in a way. He would kiss me at the door, but somehow we ended up on my couch, his body covering mine, his mouth claiming mine, and his hands doing crazy-insane things to my body. Just thinking about it now, as I rolled the pen between my hands, created a heady rush of sensations. I flushed and my body responded as I remembered how his hand felt between my thighs and how easily his skilled caresses worked my body into a frenzy.

And he always stopped before either of us found any release. He was an expert tease. Or maybe he just didn't want to go that far and—I cut that thought off, slapping it away like it was nothing more than a worrisome fly. That thought didn't even make sense. It was stupid.

I was done with being stupid.

Besides, things were already progressing crazy fast between us. It made sense that some area of our relationship would be slowed down, which is basically what he'd said. I could and did respect that, and part of me was glad that there was something holding us back. Deep down, I knew I wasn't ready for that. Well, my body was. I had a feeling that what beat strongly in my chest was also on board, but my head...my head had a hard time letting go of the noxious, poisonous whispers.

I'd never thought of myself as someone who had self-esteem issues. I had my body hang-ups, like any normal woman, but the lack of intimacy and the reintroduction of it shined a really harsh light on the way I viewed myself, on how unconnected I was with my own body.

The way Colton looked at me, how he touched me, drew my focus back to myself. He probably would have no idea what that meant for me...or probably what that was *doing* to me.

I placed the pen back in the coffee cup an author had sent me, pulse pounding in all the interesting, distracting places. It was Sunday and we'd made plans to see each other this evening, nothing further or more concrete than that, and I was still edgy with anticipation.

To be honest, I wasn't sure I ever felt any of this with Kevin. Not because my feelings for him were weaker, because they weren't, but we'd gotten together so young. What I felt then was nothing like what I felt now, and maybe if Kevin and I had met when we were older, I would be experiencing this with him.

All the maddening rush of emotions was a bit too much to handle. It was like seeing only in black and white, and suddenly everything was in vibrant colors. My stomach dipped as a thread of realization weaved its way through my thoughts.

Was what I was feeling something more powerful than lust and the excitement that came with new relationships? Was it love?

I swallowed hard as I turned from the dry erase board, my gaze crawling over the spines of the books I'd edited while in New York and from freelancing, but I really didn't see any of the titles.

Had I already fallen in love with Colton?

That sounded so, so ridiculous. We'd only come back into each other's lives a week ago, and we really hadn't been in each other's lives before. Not really. But what I was feeling was powerful, reminiscent of what I felt for Kevin.

It was strange to think about him while thinking about the four-letter word and Colton, all in the same sentence. It wasn't a bad feeling, like it was wrong or anything, but just odd.

Tucking my hair back behind my ears, I pressed my lips together. It wasn't like I never wanted to fall in love again. I had hoped that I would, but it wasn't something I had imagined happening in a long time. For one thing, I really didn't put myself out there to even meet anyone. To do that, I'd actually have to go out more often.

Feeling what I was caught me off guard for multiple reasons. I wasn't expecting anyone to waltz into my life, especially not Colton Anders. I wasn't expecting to feel this strongly, and although many of the books I'd edited featured characters falling in love hard and fast, I hadn't believed it was possible. Insta-love didn't exist in the real world.

Or maybe it did exist and I was actually experiencing it.

The flutter in my stomach increased. A twisty mixture of thoughts and emotions invaded me. Falling in love was exhilarating. It was arousing, possibly the most powerful aphrodisiac.

It was also scary as hell.

Because I'd already loved and lost once.

And knowing what I knew now, that I would lose Kevin, I still wouldn't go back and change a damn thing. Love, no matter the amount of pain it could rain down on your head, was worth it.

Then that meant if what I was feeling now was real, no matter how crazy it sounded and felt, it was also worth the possibility it wasn't returned, that it would never grow into something mutual, that it would cut deep in the end.

No matter what, I wasn't going to hide from what I was feeling. What happened to Kevin and what I'd seen Friday night proved that life was truly too short to not live it.

To be a coward.

Walking into my bedroom, I kicked off my flip-flops as I glanced at the dress I planned to wear tonight. It wasn't fancy, just a cotton eyelet pattern dress, but I was trying to get more comfortable in my own skin. Reaching down, pulling my shirt off, cool air washed over my breasts and the already hardened nipples tingled sharply. As I pulled off my bottoms, I couldn't help but imagine Colton doing it. I could easily see him on his knees, staring up at me with those ocean-blue eyes.

My stomach hallowed as I sat on the edge of my bed. I needed to shower and get ready, but my hand floated to the base of my throat. There was a moment of hesitation as I bit down on my lower lip. I knew what my body wanted—what I wanted. The tension had been building all week and I felt like I was going to crawl out of my skin.

Getting off had been kind of clinical in the past, almost as if I was detached from what I was doing and feeling. It was just about feeling a few moments of pleasure, but this, right now, was so much more potent. My hand trembled as I realized what I wanted to do and this time, it was so different.

The sharp swirl of pleasure built as I drew my hand down. My arm brushed over the tip of my breast, causing me to suck in a shallow breath. I wasn't thinking as I dragged my fingers down, my nails scrapping lightly over the puckered nipple. Colton consumed my thoughts as my hand drifted down my stomach, beyond my navel. The moment my fingers brushed through the gathering wetness, a breathy moan escaped me. I slipped a finger in as I pressed the palm of my hand against the nub of nerves.

Pleasure pounded, heavy and intense. I let myself fall back against the bed as I widened my legs. My eyes were opened into thin slits. I could see the tips of my breasts, the curve of my stomach, and my hand moving between my thighs.

I'd never watched myself before, but I couldn't look away this time, and my heart thumped fast as I lifted my hips, meeting the thrust of my finger. There was something wholly erotic about this—about watching what I was doing.

My breathing turned shallow, and in an instant, I saw Colton's head bowed between my thighs instead of my hand, and it was his fingers instead of mine, his mouth. The tension coiled and then unraveled without warning, whipping throughout me. I kicked my head back, crying out in the silence of my bedroom. The release was more intense than anytime I'd ever done this, shocking me.

Closing my eyes, I let out a long sigh as I slowly pulled my hand away, letting it rest on my belly. God, my hormones were out of control.

Actually, my emotions were out of control, but in a very good way. My lips curved up at the corners, forming a small, sated smile. I blinked open my eyes, my gaze focusing on the ceiling. My muscles were nothing and moving from this bed was the last thing I wanted, but I...

I felt...alive.

* * * *

Colton really did know the way to my heart.

Crab rangoons.

When he showed up Sunday evening, he'd brought a delicious array of takeout, including my weakness, which existed in the form of crab and cream cheese. He'd also brought a movie with him since I'd replaced the TV a few days ago. It wasn't nearly as nice or as big as the first one, but it would have to do until I could justify spending hundreds of dollars on a larger TV. He'd brought with him a remake of an old-school horror film that had traumatized me as a small child, and when we finished dinner, he popped the movie in.

We started off sitting side by side, but before we were even fifteen minutes into the movie, Colton stretched out his long body across the couch. He managed to coax me down so I was lying beside him, my head tucked against his arm and his hand resting lightly on my hip.

At that point, I pretty much stopped watching the movie.

Kevin and I had done this so many times, favoring bumming around the house many Saturday nights instead of going out. I expected there to be a pang of sorrow, but what I felt was a shadow of the hurt I had lived with in the months and even years after his death. I knew beyond a doubt that if Kevin was aware of what I was doing right now with Colton, he would be happy. Knowing that made it easy to relax against Colton.

But that relaxation quickly turned to keen awareness. With every breath Colton took, I was conscious of just how close we were. The scene of a screaming girl on the TV became nothing more than background noise as I focused on every part of our bodies that touched. The front of his thighs pressed against the back of mine. My bottom was almost cradled in his lap and his hard chest was against my back. I bit down on my lip as I wiggled a little, stopping the moment his fingers of the hand resting on my hip curled, bunching the thin material of the dress.

I thought about what I had done this afternoon, touching myself while thinking of him, and my body flushed hot. Not from embarrassment, but from sharp arousal.

"Are you watching the movie?" Colton asked, his voice deeper, rougher.

I had a choice. I could pretend that I was or I could fess up to the fact I had absolutely no interest in the movie at the moment and that it was him who had my attention. It wasn't…easy to initiate this. My seduction skills were below amateur level, but what had I decided earlier? Not to be a coward. To live life despite the risk of getting hurt. To…to just let go.

Before I could give myself time to overthink, I shifted onto my back and lifted my gaze to his. Our eyes held for a moment and then his gaze dropped to my mouth. I knew that whatever I would say would probably be completely idiotic. I decided action was probably better than words.

Because words could be really hard.

I lifted my hand, pressing my palm against his clean-shaven cheek. My heart stuttered as he turned his head slightly, dropping a kiss against the center of my hand. Oh God, that was too sweet, almost too much. I started to pull my hand away, but I stopped myself as his gaze returned to mine. Drawing in a shallow breath, I guided his mouth to mine.

I kissed him, and I don't know if he could read minds or if he really was a damn unicorn, but he let me set the pace, allowed me to play. I mapped out his mouth, covering every delectable centimeter, and when I wanted more, he opened his mouth to my searching kiss. I leisurely explored him, breathing in the taste of him.

Far too immersed in the sensations kissing him created, I wholeheartedly welcomed the moment he took over. His lips were demanding, and I yielded to him, letting out a breathless moan against his hot mouth as his hand *finally* moved from my hip, smoothing up over my breast. I sucked in a sharp breath. The dress had a built-in bra, and the thin cotton was no barrier against the heat of his hand.

I moaned into his mouth as his hand closed over my breast and kneaded gently. His chest rumbled against my side. "God, we're not even twenty minutes into the movie."

A tiny laugh escaped me. "Is that a bad thing?"

"Hell, do you even have to ask that?" His deft fingers found my pebbled nipple through the dress. Liquid fire poured through me. "I like to think it's a damn good thing."

I gasped for air. "I…I like the sound of that."

"You do?" He shifted so his weight rested on his left arm as his right hand slipped under the neckline of my dress. My back arched. "Yeah, you do."

"I do," I admitted.

He lowered his mouth to mine once more, kissing me. "I don't think I can do the gentleman thing any longer. I want to touch you." His fingers plucked at my nipple, wringing a cry out of me. "But I really want to touch you elsewhere."

My body shuddered. I had a good idea that I knew where "elsewhere" was. I closed my eyes and whispered, "I want that too."

"Thank God." His hand left my breast, and I nearly ached from the loss, but his hand was on the move again, smoothing down my stomach.

I blinked open my eyes, watching as he glided down my stomach, over my thigh. My breath lodged in my throat as he worked his hand under the skirt of my dress. I bit down on my lip as I gripped his arm. His gaze flicked to mine. "Don't stop," I said.

"No?" He kissed me, nipping at my lip as he lifted his head. When I shook my head, he fused our mouths together. His hand skated up my bare thigh, and then over the lacy edge of my panties.

I held my breath, partly due to the swirling pleasure building inside of me and I knew he could feel just how soft I was. There wasn't an ounce of hardness to my thighs or my hips. He didn't seem to notice or care, because his hand had made its way underneath my panties.

My hand tightened around his arm as his fingers reached the apex of my thighs. He brushed his lips over mine. "Open for me?"

Never in my life had there been three words that were hotter than that. My thighs parted, and his finger skimmed over my damp skin. The touch was barely there, but I jerked nonetheless.

"So sensitive," he murmured. "I like that."

My heart was pounding as he ran a lazy finger over my wet center and then he eased one finger in. A low sound worked its way out of me, and when his thumb pressed down on the buddle of nerves, I gasped out, "Colton."

His mouth covered mine as fierce heat surfaced, building and building until I was sure I would combust. My hips bucked against his hand and blood pounded, creating a ringing in my ears.

No. Wait. That wasn't in my ears. It was a phone—Colton's phone. He ignored it—thank God—as he worked his finger in and out, devouring me with kisses. The tension coiled and I suddenly wanted, needed, to feel his skin against mine. I grabbed a fistful of his shirt, yanking it up. His body jerked and he made a harsh sound the second my hand touched the hard planes of his stomach.

Good God, there wasn't an ounce of *him* that was soft. My eager fingers traced each tightly packed ab. My hand dipped, brushing the button on his jeans.

The phone started ringing again, a few seconds after it had ended, and this time, Colton's hand stilled between my thighs. I almost prayed he didn't stop, but he did.

Groaning, he lifted his head and glanced over at where his phone rested on the coffee table. His hand slipped away from me. "It's work. I'm sorry."

"It's okay," I murmured, dazed by the rioting sensations in my body.

Rolling over me in one fluid move, he snatched up his phone and stood. "It's Anders." There was a pause. "Yeah, I couldn't get to my phone. What's up?"

I looked over at him, clearly seeing the hard ridge of his erection straining against his jeans.

Damn, what a waste.

I suddenly wanted to giggle, except I saw Colton stiffen and caught a brief glimpse of a frown as he turned away from me. He picked up the remote, pausing the movie. "Yeah, you know where I'm at."

My brows knitted.

Colton glanced back at me, his expression inscrutable. "Are you serious? Hell." He shook his head, glancing at the now repaired window. "I'm not surprised, but didn't think it would happen this quickly."

Glancing down, I saw that the skirt of my dress was hiked up to my hips, revealing the black undies. Face flushing red, I hastily reached down and fixed it. Then I figured I should sit up.

"You need me in tonight?" he asked, and I worried my lower lip, hoping nothing serious had happened, which was a stupid thought. Colton was a detective. Serious stuff happened all the time. "Shit. Yeah, that's good and that's bad."

My gaze shot to him as icy motion stabbed my stomach.

"Okay. I'll see you tomorrow." Colton disconnected the call and placed it back on the table. Sitting down beside me, he exhaled slowly. "Sorry about that. It was my partner—Hart."

The cold feeling was still there. "That's okay. Your job is important. When you get a call, you have to answer."

"I do." He rested his hands on his knees. "I have kind of good news."

"Kind of?"

Colton nodded. "We've identified one of the two men you saw last Friday." He paused, his jaw hardening. "There's no easy way to say this. Apparently he was pulled from Schuylkill River."

I stiffened, eyes widening. "What?"

"One of the men you saw that night is dead, Abby."

Chapter 11

All the heat vanished and a different kind of tension built in the pit of my stomach. At first, I didn't think I heard him right. The bomb he dropped came out of nowhere.

I said the first thing that came to mind. "Are you sure?"

And that was a dumb question.

He nodded. "It's not the man who did the shooting. It appears to be the other suspect."

Leaning back against the cushion, I tucked my legs under me as I tried to process what had just happened. My thoughts were running in so many different directions. Not the man who pulled the trigger—the one with the cold, dead eyes? "How did he die?"

Colton twisted his body toward me. "Sweetheart, that's not something you need to know."

Part of me wanted to know, as morbid as that sounded. "But how?"

He glanced at the paused movie. "Remember when I told you about Isaiah Vakhrov?"

The mob guy. How could I forget him? I nodded.

"As far as I know right now, there's no evidence pointing to him having a hand in this, but I'd be willing to bet my retirement it was him." Colton lifted his hand, sighing as he scrubbed his fingers through his hair. "It's messed up, you know? These guys have their set of moral codes, twisted moral codes, and while those guys killed someone, murdering them isn't the answer."

"Agreed," I whispered, shivering. "I…I don't even know what to say."

"There's really nothing to say, but with the one dead, the shooter is probably going to be on the run. If he's smart that is."

My gaze flipped to his as pressure squeezed my chest. "What about the guys who warned me in the parking lot? They won't think I ratted their guys out?"

His jaw hardened as his gaze turned icy. "They'd have to be fucking idiots to think you had anything to do with this."

But they had been idiotic enough to approach me in the first place. Another shiver tiptoed its way over my shoulders. I hadn't forgotten about them or the fear they'd induced this past week. It was just something I tried not to think about. I didn't like the idea of living with that kind of fear.

Maybe that wasn't wise.

"There's one more thing. Hart was able to pull some more photos of those who match your description of the shooter," he explained. "We'd like you to look at them as soon as possible."

I nodded again.

Colton reached over, placing the tips of his fingers under my chin. He lifted my gaze to his. "I'm going to make sure you're safe, Abby."

"Is that why you've been spending so much time with me?" The moment that question left my mouth, I wanted to dropkick myself in the face. I couldn't even believe those words came out of me. It was like they existed in a dark, stupid as hell place that I had no control over.

His brows lifted as he stared at me. "Come again?"

Oh God. My cheeks heated. "I mean, I know I'm a witness and keeping me safe is a part of your job, but I…" I mentally strung together an epic amount of curse words. "I don't even know what I'm saying."

Colton dropped his hand. "I think you kind of do, Abby."

Uncurling my legs, I nervously smoothed my hands over the skirt of my dress. Was my question a Freudian slip in a way? Of course it was. Because that stupid as hell, ugly part of me still couldn't fathom Colton being here because he was sincerely attracted to me, even after what had just gone down between us.

I was an idiot.

His eyes narrowed. "Do you really think that me being here has to do with what happened last Friday?"

"Well, that's how we crossed paths—"

"You know that's not what I'm getting at," he interrupted. "And I know that's not what you were trying to say. You think I'm here, with you, with some kind of ulterior motive?"

A sick feeling expanded in my chest. "I don't think…" I trailed off because if I was being honest with myself, I was lying.

"I'll do anything to keep a witness safe and to get the job done," he said, shaking his head. "But I wouldn't go that damn far, Abby. I'm here and have been here with you simply because I want to be. I'd think the fact that I had my hand between your thighs ten minutes ago would be proof enough of that."

Warmth infused my cheeks as I bit down on the inside of my cheek. A moment passed. "I'm sorry. I didn't mean to insinuate anything."

"You don't need to apologize."

It was my turn to shake my head because I did need to apologize. "But I do, because…because saying something like that isn't saying great things about you as a person." I let out a long breath. What could I say? That I was trying to improve my confidence? That I just… "I'm stupid."

One eyebrow rose. "You're not stupid. That's not the problem."

A slice of unease lit up my chest as I glanced at him. He was staring straight ahead, his gaze fixed on the wall. A numbness settled in the pit of my stomach.

His shoulders tensed. "You're a beautiful woman, Abby. And you're smart and kind. You're funny." He turned to me, a distant gleam in his eyes. "And it's a damn shame you don't see that."

The numbness spread like icy drizzle, coating my skin. Underneath it, embarrassment burned. Were my hang-ups that obvious? I squeezed my eyes shut. *God, this was humiliating.*

"I'm going to…I'm going to go ahead and head out," he said, and my eyes snapped open. He was staring at the wall again as disappointment, remorse, and a hundred other messy emotions churned inside me. "Keep the movie. We'll watch it later."

A knot formed in the base of my throat. For some reason, I didn't think "later" was going to come soon.

"Okay?" he asked.

Pressing my lips together, I nodded as he rose and then I forced a smile when he bent over, pressing his lips against my forehead. My chest squeezed at the sweet gesture, and somehow I managed to walk him to the door and to say good-bye. And when I closed the door, I leaned against it, pressing my balled hands against my eyes.

The sick feeling expanded, circling my heart. There was a good chance that in such a short period of time, I'd fallen for Colton and I...I might have already lost him.

Chapter 12

Colton had texted Monday morning asking if I could stop by the office today to look at the photos again, but when I got there, he wasn't there. I tried not to take it personally as I was handed off to Detective Hart and taken into a private room, but it was hard. My stomach churned as Detective Hart spread glossy photographs across the scratched surface of the table.

I wanted to ask where Colton was. Hell, I wanted to whip out my phone and text him. Call him.

"Just take your time," he said, sitting back in the metal chair. "There's no rush."

My gaze flickered over the photographs as my heart started pounding in my chest. I needed to focus. Priorities. Right now, what had happened with Colton wasn't the most important thing going on.

The shooter was still out there.

Taking my time, I looked at each of the photos spread out in front of me. At first, they all looked alike—men in their upper twenties, bald with tats on the neck or just on their arms. I'd looked at twenty or so before Detective Hart added five more photos to the mix. I glanced over at them.

My heart stopped as I sucked in an unsteady breath. I reached over, picking up the third photograph, and held it close. There were three shots: full frontal and two profiles.

"Ms. Ramsey?"

For a moment I couldn't get my tongue to work. Like it was glued to the roof of my mouth. My hand trembled as I stared at the face of the man I'd seen shoot someone—kill someone. My throat was dry. "It's him."

Detective Hart leaned forward, placing his forearm on the table. "Are you sure?"

"Positive." I cleared my throat. "That's him." Unable to look at the photo any longer, I handed it over to the detective. Satisfaction gleamed in his eyes. "What's his name?" I asked and then frowned. "You probably can't tell me that, can you?"

He slipped the photo in a file. "You'd be correct. At least not right now." Standing, he reached into his pocket and pulled out his phone. "There's just a couple of forms we need you to sign and then you'll be on your way."

Taking several shallow breaths, I ignored the unease twisting up my insides. Detective Hart paused at the door. "You're going to put this man behind bars, where he belongs." His smile was tight. "And you've probably saved his life."

* * * *

Monday was weird.

I couldn't focus on the new manuscript, not that anyone would blame me. I'd identified a murderer this morning and according to Detective Hart, I'd probably saved his life by doing so. Unless the mob guy Colton had mentioned got to him first.

Colton.

Throughout the day, I engaged in some major wishful phone checking. As if somehow I had missed his text or call. Of course, there were no missed messages. My stomach dropped. After identifying the shooter, I figured Colton would be in contact, even if it was in a purely professional sense.

Monday slowly churned into Tuesday. No calls. No texts. I could've messaged him, I realized that, but I was the one who messed up and I honestly had no experience in these things. Dating was so far out of my realm of understanding. Was I supposed to give him space? Give him time? Or was he waiting for me to reach out? Or was he just really busy? The latter made sense. He was probably trying to search down the shooter.

Sitting at my desk, I groaned as I leaned over, resting my forehead against the cool wood. I was such an idiot. I'd let that stupid, ugly voice in my head get the better of me. I was still letting it get the better of me, wasn't I? Because why hadn't I messaged Colton?

Messaging Colton would be the normal thing to do.

I lifted my head and gently lowered it back to the desk. Rinse and repeat. What was I doing, other than banging my head on a desk? Because that wasn't weird or anything. Okay. I needed a plan. My heart skipped a beat when I lifted my head and saw my cell. I could text him, something small. I could totally do it.

Snatching up my phone, I tapped the screen and then the little green message icon. My pulse was kicking around as I hit Colton's name and started typing out the first thing that came to mind. I didn't let myself stop and think about it or let myself feel stupid for typing it out. The message was just four words.

I miss your crepes.

Okay. That was kind of a cute message and sort of stupid. A lot stupid. Before I hit send, I deleted the message.

I was such an idiot, geez.

I didn't text Colton and I didn't hear from him.

My life had been so crazy the last two weeks it was almost hard to believe that only that short amount of time had passed. I didn't know how to feel about witnessing a murder, knowing one was dead, and the other one, the shooter, would soon be—hopefully—apprehended.

I didn't know how to feel about a lot of things.

Actually, that wasn't entirely true. When it came to Colton, I knew exactly how I felt. Crappy. I didn't think his text Monday was an excuse to not see me. After all, after what happened, he would be busy, and since he normally worked on Tuesday, I wasn't expecting a visit.

I didn't get one either.

And he hadn't texted or called. There was a part of me that wanted to listen to the small and probably more reasonable voice that claimed his lack of contact didn't mean anything. He had to be busy, and I also hadn't reached out to him. Mainly because I didn't know what to say.

I still couldn't believe I had asked him that question. If he was angry, which I knew he had been even though he'd said I hadn't needed to apologize, it was within his right. Insinuating that he had some kind of ulterior motive to spending time with me and doing the things we had been doing was downright insulting.

I'd fucked up.

And as Jillian sat on the edge of my couch early Wednesday evening, watching me pace back and forth in my living room, I told her just how badly I'd fucked up while she sipped the latte she'd brought with her.

"So, that's about it." I dropped down on the couch, eyeing the cappuccino she'd brought me. It was all gone. "Not only does he probably think I'm a jackass, he also knows I have the confidence of a sewer rat."

Jillian frowned from behind the rim of her cup. "I don't think he believes you're an asshole. He told you not to apologize."

"That's because he's a good guy and he's not mean to anyone. Even in high school he was that way. Standing up for the kids that got picked on and friendly to everyone, and this last week has taught me he hasn't changed in that department." I grabbed the empty cup and stood, unable to stay seated. I walked into the kitchen, tossing it in the trash. "If he thought I was a jackass, he's not going to say anything."

"That may be true, but I just don't think that's the case." She placed her cup on the coffee table and waited until I returned to the living room. "And about the confidence thing? You shouldn't be embarrassed by it."

Stopping near the TV, I arched a brow as I folded my arms across my chest. "Lack of confidence is seriously one of the most unattractive things out there."

Jillian rolled her eyes. "And it's also seriously one of the most normal, common things out there."

"True," I murmured.

"I always thought being told you should be more confident, because confidence is sexy, was like getting a bitch slap in the face," Jillian said. "Like 'thanks for pointing that out.'"

I laughed dryly. "It's weird, you know? I hadn't even noticed this about myself in the last couple of years. I just sort of stopped thinking about myself as a woman. I know that sounds stupid, but that's the best way I can explain it. I think..." I sat back down, resting my hands in my lap as I gave a lopsided shrug. "And I was always so comfortable with Kevin. It wasn't something I ever had to think about, and I think the newness of all of this rattled me."

"That's understandable."

A weak smile crossed my lips as I glanced at my phone. Colton should be off tonight, unless he was still handling the investigation. My stomach dropped a little. "I guess in a way it's a blessing in disguise. At least now I know how I feel. I can do something about it."

She twisted toward me. Thick brown hair slid off her shoulder as she tilted her head to the side. "Like what?"

I really wasn't going to admit to the whole staring at myself naked thing. "Mostly I think I just need to be more aware of myself. Take some time for myself, you know?"

"You do work all the time," she agreed after a moment. "I thought my dad worked a lot, but I think the only time you take off is when we get together."

That would be an affirmative.

She peeked at me through the thick fringe of bangs. "Do you...want to change yourself?"

"Who doesn't want to change themselves, just a little bit?" I laughed as I brushed my hair back behind my ear. "I mean, I could probably be a wee bit healthier. Stop drinking cappuccinos every day. But I'd rather be happy with myself than to really try to change everything about myself."

"That's good." Her gaze lowered. "I wish I thought that. About myself, I mean."

I frowned. "Do you want to change yourself?" When she didn't answer, understanding set in. "Is that why you're transferring colleges? To start over?"

Her shoulder rose in a halfhearted shrug. "I just want to...yeah, I want to start over, and I can. I will."

Concern flickered through me. I reached over, placing my hand on her arm. "Is everything okay?"

Jillian nodded in response to the loaded question. The girl had never been very forthcoming with information, only dropping bits and pieces here and there. I knew she wasn't close to many people, except…except a guy named Brock. He was some kind of fighter with her father's organization. From what I had gathered, he'd been around her family for a long time.

And whenever she did talk about him, which wasn't often, her face would always get this look of absolute adoration on it.

"Jillian—"

"I just don't want to end up doing what my entire family does. Everything is about the Academy, and that's not what I want to do. The only way I'm going to escape that is by leaving now. Anyway," she said, pursing her lips as a thoughtful look crossed her face. "One of the things you never really see in a romance book is a woman who has self-esteem issues. I mean, I'm sure they're out there, but they're few and far between. Like they can have eating disorders, post-traumatic stress from sexual assault or mental abuse. They can be sold into sex trafficking and they can carry epic amounts of grief. We have female characters who have suffered every loss imaginable and ones who are scarred physically and mentality, but where in the hell are the average women? Ones who look in the mirror and cringe a little? Like, why are all those others acceptable to women, but reading or knowing another woman who has a low self-esteem is, like, worse than all that drama llama? Dude, I get reading for wish fulfillment, but you've got to have a little reality in the story."

Brushing her bangs out of her eyes, Jillian exhaled loudly and then continued. "Whatever. It doesn't matter. You're normal. I'm normal. We're not perfect and not having the greatest confidence doesn't make you any less of a person."

What Jillian said was so true.

Holy crap, the raw truth of it all floored me.

Women wanted other women to have high self-esteem and confidence. No one wanted to ever admit that their confidence was lacking, that they had a hard time looking at themselves in the mirror.

It was wrong that we weren't able to have our weak moments. That we had to hide the fact that we were uncomfortable with our imperfections. That the journey to loving yourself doesn't exclude recognizing there were days when you just didn't want to see yourself naked.

And that there were worse things than having some confidence issues.

I glanced over at Jillian. This was one of those moments when I forgot that she was so young, because damn, she really could be a hell of a lot wiser than me. "You're right."

Her face transformed prettily when she smiled. "I know."

I laughed. "And modest."

"Whatever." Leaning forward, she smacked her hands off her knees. "Do you want to go out?"

"Go where?"

"I don't know. You live pretty close to the bar near Outback."

"Mona's?" I started to grin. "Jillian, I don't think you're allowed to go there."

"I've been there before. As long as they don't serve me, Jax is cool with it."

My brows rose. "Jax?"

"He's the owner. He's good friends with Brock." She stood.

I eyed her. "So…is Brock going to be there?"

"I doubt it," she said. "He's usually training now."

For some reason I didn't quite believe her.

"Come on. It'll be good to get out." She paused. "Plus, you know who's the bartender there, right?"

It took a second to click. "Wait. That's where Roxy works and she's dating…"

"Colton's brother," she finished.

The tumbling in my stomach this time was something altogether different. "How do you know that?"

She rolled her eyes again. "Brock is really good friends with all of them and I'm a really good…listener. So, you want to go? I'll be good and order a Coke."

I shot her a look. "Wild child."

Jillian giggled, and I had to grin because I wasn't sure I'd ever heard her giggle. "So?"

Glancing at the clock, I saw it was still early. I'd planned on cracking open the new manuscript I'd received, but wasn't I supposed to start taking more time to myself? And besides, if I stayed home, all I would do is end up staring at my phone, engaging in wishful thinking.

"Okay," I said, standing up. "Let's do it."

* * * *

It had been about a year since I'd been in Mona's, and while the bar had a dive feel to it, it wasn't a creepy place. Jillian and I took our own cars since she lived in the opposite direction, closer to the city.

The moment I saw Jax, I remembered who he was. How could I have forgotten? Even though he was a few years younger than me, he was the kind of man who gave off the vibe that said he knew how to take care of things.

He was behind the bar when I led the way to a table. Since Jillian was underage, she couldn't sit at the bar. Jax had the greatest smile and laugh, which he handed out freely. Right now, he was laughing at something someone was saying at the bar. Tipping his head back and letting loose a deep, infectious laugh.

"You just want a Coke? Anything to eat?" I asked.

Jillian was scanning the heads bowed over one of the pool tables. "Nah. Coke is fine."

There weren't a lot of people at the bar when I walked over to it, so the girl behind it quickly came to where I stood. I knew who she was. This was Roxy—Reece's girlfriend. As she drew nearer, I saw that she had a streak of color in her brown hair that matched her purple glasses. Envy filled me. I always wanted to have a wild color in my hair, but I didn't have the face or the personality to pull that off.

Her shirt read *I'm like a self-cleaning oven*, and under it was a happy little oven, and then below that were the words *I'm self-sufficient, bitches*.

I wanted that shirt.

"What can I get…?" Roxy's hazel eyes widened behind the glasses. "Hey, how are you?"

Shocked that she recognized me, I floundered for a moment. "Good. I'm good. You?"

"Great. I haven't seen you in a while. Wow. It's been forever." She leaned against the bar, grinning. "I wasn't even sure you still lived around here." The door opened and a group rolled in, heading toward the bar. "What can I get you?"

"Just two Cokes." I paused. "And a menu."

Roxy nodded. "Coming right up."

I glanced over at the table. Jillian was staring down at her phone, her fingers flying a mile a minute.

"I'm giving them another minute, and if he's not out, I'm going in," I heard Jax say as he reached around Roxy, grabbing a bottle of liquor.

"For rescue?" she replied, her brows raising as she scooped ice into two glasses.

"Hmm," he grunted, screwing off the lid.

"I have no idea what's going on there. I thought they weren't together," she said, placing the two glasses in front of me. She grabbed a menu as she looked over her shoulder at Jax. "He needs to hurry up anyways. Reece has already texted asking where his brother is."

My heart stopped. They were talking about Colton. Holy crap. Okay, there was a tiny part of me that hoped he'd be here but also was terrified of the fact if he was, because then that meant he wasn't at work. And he hadn't gotten in contact with me.

And I hadn't gotten in contact with him either.

And it didn't sound like he was alone.

"Here you go." Roxy smiled as she placed the menu down.

I numbly handed over the cash, and had just picked up the glasses, along with the menu, when I saw him.

He appeared on the other side of the bar, and even from where I stood, I could see that his jaw was a hard line. My heart started racing. I tightened my hands on the glasses. Roxy said something, but I really didn't hear her.

Then I saw *her*.

The tall blonde I'd seen him with before. She was as gorgeous as I remembered. Hair shiny and straight, well past her shoulders, and she was thin. Like I would probably hurt her if I sat on her level of thin. Blood drained from my face as I realized who this woman was. In my heart of hearts I knew it was her, his ex-fiancée.

Oh my God.

"I was getting worried about you," Jax said, placing the bottle back.

Colton glanced over at him, and his gaze was icy as it moved past Jax and Roxy and then over me. He stopped. Literally stopped walking, jerking to a halt.

Our eyes met, and I couldn't even think. There were no thoughts as we stared at each other. My heart…it felt like it stopped, just like him.

"Um," Roxy murmured.

The woman with Colton said something. Her bow-shaped lips moved, but he didn't react. Not at first, and then he did.

"Shit," he said, and he turned to the stunning blonde, who had placed her hand on his arm. The touch was familiar, as if she had done it a thousand times before.

I whipped around, my skin tingling as I walked the drinks and menu to the table. I put them down before I dropped them.

"Are you ok…oh my God." Jillian's eyes doubled in size.

The twisting in my stomach made me nauseous as I flushed hot and then cold. "I think—" I shook my head, my cheeks burning. "God, I'm so sorry, but I really need to go."

Jillian rose, sympathy crossing her face. "Oh my gosh, I'm sorry. I didn't think something like this would—"

"I know." A knot formed in my throat, and the ache pouring into my chest told me that what I felt for Colton was not simply like or attraction. "I hate to do this." Pressing my lips together, I breathed out of my nose. "This is so embarrassing."

"It's okay." She squeezed my arm. "Go. Just call me when you get there, okay?"

Nodding, I bent down and kissed her cheek, then I grabbed my purse. I didn't dare look back as I headed for the door, and I knew even as I yanked it open, I was being such a coward.

My confidence sucked and I was a coward. Great. Winning combination. I didn't remember much of the drive home and as I walked inside, I kicked off the heels and left them just inside the door.

After I texted Jillian, I felt horrible. I shouldn't have bolted. I should've sat there and pretended like what the fuck ever. Tossing my phone on the couch, I pressed my palm against my forehead. The whole being an idiot thing was a running theme.

But Colton had been there with the same beautiful blonde. The fiancée—ex-fiancée, and Sunday, he had been kissing me, touching me, and telling me that I was beautiful and smart, and tonight he was with her?

What in the hell?

Anger surfaced, and I dug my phone out from between the cushions of my couch. I didn't even know what I was going to do. Text him? Call? Throw my phone? All seemed like a viable option.

A knock at the door stopped me.

I turned around and for a moment I didn't move. Despite the fact I'd just seen Colton with her, hope sparked deep in my chest, and how incredibly stupid was that? I doubted they just happened to run into each other. Then again, it had been purely coincidental that I'd even been there.

I shouldn't have left.

The knock came again, and my feet came unglued from the floor. With my phone in one hand, I opened the door.

It happened so fast.

A shadow—*a person*—shoved inside, slamming the door against the wall. There was a glimpse of a band of dark ink around thick biceps. A scream built in my throat and ripped loose a second before pain exploded along the side of my head, stunning me.

I stumbled to the side, my phone slipping from my fingers and hitting the floor. A door slammed shut and a second later, the wind was knocked out of me as my back hit the floor. My lungs seized as I stared up.

It was *him*—the shooter.

Holy shit.

Had he pistol-whipped me? Wet warmth trickled down the side of my neck. The whole left side of my head throbbed.

A fine sheen of sweat dotted his forehead as he towered over me, a gun in his hand. "You couldn't keep your fucking mouth shut, could you?"

My heart lodged in my throat as I scrambled backward, my hands slipping over the wood floors. A flip-flop came off as I reached the edge of the throw carpet.

He followed me. "All you had to do was keep your fucking mouth

102/Jennifer L. Armentrout

shut. That was all. Now Mickey is dead and the son-of-a-bitch Vakhrov is gunning for me, all because you couldn't keep your cunt mouth shut."

My vision blurred a little as I tried to remember who Mickey was. It took a moment for my brain to process the fact that Mickey must be the other man I'd seen him with. "I... I didn't identify hi—"

"Shut up! Shut the fuck up!" He shouted, his finger twitching over the trigger of the gun he held. "You're going to tell me you didn't say shit? Because Mickey is dead and the Goddamn police raided my momma's house yesterday."

I scooted back against the wall, my heart pounding so fast I thought I'd be sick. This was so bad, so freaking bad I could barely process what was happening. The only thing I knew was that I was staring death in the eyes.

His lip curled, just like it had right before he'd shot that man. "Stupid bitch. Lift your hands."

Swallowing hard, I raised my shaking hands as my thoughts raced. I had no idea how to get out of this. Could I reason with him?

His dark eyes held a certain glassy sheen to them and his pupils were way too dilated as he jerked the gun at me. "Stand up." When I didn't move, he screamed, "Stand the fuck up!"

Okay. I was standing.

Slowly, I pushed to my feet, losing the other flip-flop in the process. "We can work this—"

"Shut. Up." He stepped forward. "What part of that do you not understand? There's nothing—"

The muted sound of sirens silenced him. Hope exploded in my stomach. Had someone—one of my neighbors—heard my scream and his yelling?

I really needed to thank my neighbors. Bake them a cake or something. If I actually lived through this.

He heard the sirens, and in seconds, the whirling noise grew closer and louder. "Shit. Fuck. Damn."

My wide gaze darted across the room, searching for some kind of weapon. Unless I could grab a lamp before he shot me, I was screwed, but I had to try something. Through the front window, I could see flashing red and blue lights beyond the curtains. The cops were here and I seriously doubted this guy planned on walking out of here alive or letting me go.

Sudden shouts from the front of the house erupted, and horror settled in as I recognized one of the voices. No. No. No.

A loud knock on the door caused me to jump, sending a wave of dizziness through me. "Abby? You in there?" a voice boomed through the closed door. "It's Colton. Open the door."

Before I could open my mouth, the guy lurched forward, slamming into me. The back of my head knocked off the wall. His hand clamped down on my mouth as he got right up in my face.

"Abby!" Colton shouted, and the front door rattled as he or something slammed into it.

The man's breath stunk of stale cigarettes and booze as he pressed against me. "Fucking cops, motherfucking cops," he grunted, pressing the muzzle of the gun against the side of my head. "You say one word, I will blow your fucking brains out right now."

Right now, I thought dumbly. Versus later? A hysterical giggle climbed up my throat. The banging at the front door didn't stop, but I no longer heard Colton. How was he here? If the police were called there was no way he would've found out that quickly. It didn't make sense, but at this moment, it didn't matter.

If Colton somehow got through that door, I knew this man would shoot him. My stomach hollowed in fear.

"We're going to go out your back door, okay?" he said. "And you're going to make sure I get the hell out of here. You get me?"

Squeezing my eyes shut, I nodded. He was going to use me as some kind of shield, and I knew the moment he got outside, he was going to shoot me. It was either in here or out there, where he'd have a chance to shoot someone else—a neighbor, one of the cops, or Colton.

I couldn't let that happen.

No way.

I might have the self-esteem of a sloth, but I wasn't a coward. No. I survived my parents' death. I survived New York City. I survived my husband's death. I *survived*.

I was *not* a coward.

He grabbed ahold of my shoulder and pulled me away from the wall.

With one well-place shove in the center of my back, he guided me through the living room. Someone was yelling at the front door again, but it wasn't Colton.

"Keep quiet," he urged, and when I didn't move quickly, he shoved me again.

I stumbled into the small dining room table. The impact knocked over the heavy ceramic vase, spilling plastic flowers across the surface. The vase rolled toward me.

"Get moving," he ordered.

My gaze zeroed in on the vase. It was within grasp. Right there. My heart rate seemed to slow. Everything slowed down actually.

"Goddammit." He balled his fist in my hair and yanked my head back sharply. Pain tore down my neck, shooting into my back. "Get your fat ass fu—"

My brain clicked off as I grabbed the vase and spun around. The man cursed and he leveled the gun again, but I was fast when it counted. The gun went off just as I slammed the bottom of the vase into the side of his head. There was a sickening crunch and something warm and wet sprayed into the air and across my face. The gun went off again, just as wood splintered on the back door. It flew open just as the shooter crumbled to the floor.

Colton barreled in, dressed as he was at the bar, in jeans and a worn shirt. He had a gun aimed and his bright blue gaze took in the situation. Behind him, uniformed cops streamed in.

He took a step forward, keeping his gun on the shooter. "Abby?"

I was still holding the bloodied vase as I croaked out, "I'm not a coward."

Chapter 13

"You're becoming a repeat customer," Lenny, the repairman who'd previously replaced my broken window, said with a wry grin. He'd just finished fixing the broken back door, which ended up being an entirely new back door. Placing the bill on the TV, he started past me with his toolbox in hand. "I'm glad to see you're okay, though. I heard about it on the late evening news last night. This town is getting crazy. All the violence coming in from the city."

I smiled faintly as I followed him to the front door. "Thank you for coming out on such short notice. I really appreciate it."

"No problem," he replied, stepping outside. "If you need anything else, you know to call me."

"Thanks." I closed the door, sighing.

Turning around, I eyed the freshly plastered wall behind the dining room table. Lenny had also covered the two bullet holes. All I needed to do was match up the paint and then it would be like nothing had ever happened.

Last night felt like forever ago.

I'd spent the bulk of the night sitting in the ER, getting checked out and then answering a thousand and one police questions. Come to find out, the shooter had a name—Charles Bakerton. Didn't sound like a homicidal maniac's name, but Charles was still alive. I hadn't killed him with the well-placed vase of death swing. I was relieved to hear that. I didn't want to know what it felt like to kill someone.

Through the endless hours that had crept into early morning, Colton had remained beside me, mostly silent and very pissed-off looking. Those blue eyes were practically on fire. We didn't get a chance to talk, nothing other than the basics before he was called out. Surprisingly, Roxy and Reece had showed up at the hospital and had driven me home. That was…weird.

I was so lucky. Everyone kept telling me that. I had looked a lot worse than I was. Not even a concussion, and the crack upside the head hadn't even required stitches. A fistful of ibuprofen had taken care of that ache and the rest of the minor pains.

I could've died last night, so yeah, I was really lucky.

Moving to the couch, I started to pick up the remote when there was a knock on my front door. My stomach dropped. Placing the remote down, I went to the front window first. Totally learned my lesson last night. I peered out the front window.

It was Colton.

"Oh my, wow," I murmured, settling back on my bare feet. I didn't let my head race into fantasy land. Him showing up after what went down last night wasn't a surprise. In a daze, I slowly walked to the door and opened it.

His hands were planted on each side of the doorframe and he was leaning in. Blue eyes met mine. "Abby."

Somehow I plastered a smile on my face, and I had a feeling it was a crazy looking smile. "Hi, Colton!" The enthusiasm was a bit much, but I couldn't tone it down. "How are you—?"

"Don't do that," he cut in, and I felt my creeper smile wobble and then fade. "After what happened yesterday, don't pretend with me."

Well then.

He lowered his hands. "We need to talk."

We did. I stepped aside, pressing my lips together. "Come in."

Colton closed the door behind him, but instead of walking to the couch, he stopped in front of me. My breath caught as he clasped the sides of my face in a gentle grasp. His intense gaze swept over me. "How are you feeling?"

"I'm okay. Really." I forced a less weird smile. "Thanks for asking."

The skin around his eyes tensed. "I wanted to get over here earlier."

It was then when I realized he was wearing the same clothes from last night. Needless to say, he probably had a lot of...cop things going on. "It's okay. I—"

"It's not okay. It fucking killed me not to be over here. Fuck." He dropped his hands and ran one through his hair as he stepped back. "Seeing you last night, with blood on your face—fuck," he cursed again, looking away. "Damn, I said I would protect you. I didn't."

"What?" I blinked. "You couldn't have known that was going to happen. Even Detective Hart had said he figured the shooter would've run after his friend or whatever was found dead. That's not your fault."

The look on his face said he wasn't so sure of that. "He followed you to your house and he hit you with a gun. You could've died, Abby. I—"

"Colton," I tried again. "I'm serious. It wasn't your fault. Okay? And you didn't have to come over here to check on me. I'm okay. You've...you've done enough. You got your brother and Roxy to take me home and—"

"I've done enough? Obviously, I haven't done enough." His gaze found its way back to mine. "I need to make a couple of things clear. When you left Mona's last night, you were upset. I get that. You just saw me walk out with Nicole and you left before I could say a single thing to you. Don't pretend like you didn't see that."

"Okay. You, um, seemed busy." I swallowed, taking a step back. "So that...that's your ex-fiancée? She's gorgeous."

"Yeah, she is." His brows knitted as he stared down at me. "You know, I was hoping I would hear from you. I figured after Sunday, I was going to leave the ball in your court."

He had? Had he given that message through man code? I wasn't good at reading man code.

"Obviously, you need to work through some issues and I was hoping that you would let me help you with that," he continued. "I'm impatient though. I was planning on calling you last night, but my brother does this thing every week at his place—game night. It's stupid, but fun. I thought I'd swing by his place for about an hour and then call you."

I didn't know what to say about any of that, but I wasn't going to stand here like I was mute. I had a voice and I was going to use it. "But you were at Mona's, with Nicole."

"I was," he said, a muscle flexing along his jaw. "I met her there on the way to Reece's. When we broke up, there was a watch that my grandfather had given me before he passed away. One night at her place, I had taken it off and I never found it after that. Nicole finally found it." Lowering his one hand to the pocket of his denim jeans, he fished out a gold watch that looked like it cost a pretty penny. "She wanted to talk. That's why we were in Jax's office."

I stared at the watch and then watched him place it back in his pocket. Part of me felt like an idiot, but how would anyone really react in this situation? "What did she want?"

Colton didn't lie. "She misses me. That's what she wanted to talk about."

Sucking in a sharp breath, I schooled my expression blank. "Okay."

His eyes narrowed. "Is that all you have to say about that?"

The frustration rose again, rushing over my skin like an army of fiery ants. If last night had taught me anything, it was that I wasn't a coward. I was a survivor. I *really* found my voice then. "What do you want me to say, Colton? How do I respond to that? I'm not mad that she misses you. You probably miss her too. You were together for a long time, but…" My words started to fade, and while there was a part of me that just wanted to show him the door and retreat, I refused to do it. "But we just reconnected and I don't know where our relationship is going. And you know what? Yes. I don't have the greatest confidence in myself right now. I haven't seriously dated anyone besides Kevin, and the last four years have been a really long dry spell. And I know that's not the greatest issue to have, but whatever. I like you."

I'd blurted those last three words out and then I couldn't take them back. "I *really* like you, Colton. I've always liked you, but I'm going to be honest. I'm going to suck at this whole dating thing and I'm going to have moments when I doubt why you're here. And it doesn't help when your ex-fiancée looks like a *Sports Illustrated* model. I shouldn't have run from the bar. That was stupid, but guess what, I'm probably going to do a lot of stupid things. That's just the beginning."

His lips started to twitch.

My eyes narrowed. "You think this is funny?"

"No." His eyes said he was lying. "Not at all."

"Uh-huh." I folded my arms across my chest and parroted back what he'd said earlier. "Is that all you have to say about that?"

"No. That's not all." His lips did curve up at the corners then. "I don't think less of you because you don't see what I see, what I know, when I look at you. That's the issue I'm more than willing to work with. You get that?"

I nodded as I pressed my lips together.

"I like you, really like you," he repeated, and that hope in my chest sparked into a wildfire. "I've *always* liked you, too. And yeah, Nicole is great looking, but she's not the person I'm standing in front of and she's not the person who gets me hard when I think of her. And she isn't the person I almost lost last night. That's you, sweetheart, all you."

Warmth invaded my cheeks. Oh...oh wow.

"I can tell you where this relationship is going. Or at least where I hope it is. We're going to spend more time together. We're going to really get to know each other, and I'm going to chip away at that low confidence shit until you see what I see," he said, and a shiver curled along the base of my spine in response to his steely determination.

My breath caught as he took a step forward and lifted his hands, gently holding my cheeks once more. "I want this to work," he said, his voice low. "Because like I said before, I believe in second chances and I don't believe in coincidences. There was a reason why you and I reconnected, and I don't want to pass that up. And we almost lost that last night, so really, we're working on a third chance. I want this to work."

"I...I want this to work too." My heart was thumping like a steel drum.

"Then we are on the same page."

"We are," I whispered.

"Good."

Then he kissed me, and in the back of my head, I realized we were still standing just inside the foyer, but I didn't care. His kiss started off sweet and tender, but I wanted more. So did he. My hands found their way to his chest, and I could feel his heart beating just as fast as mine.

I broke the kiss, breathing heavily. "Do you want to stay?"

"Hell yeah, but if I...if I do, I'm not leaving tonight." His thumbs dragged over my cheeks. "And if I don't leave tonight, I'm going to be upstairs and I'm going to want to be in that bed and in between those pretty thighs of yours. If you don't want that or you're not up to it because of last night, let me know now. I can wait, but either way, I'm not letting go of you tonight."

"I'm *fine*." There wasn't a moment of hesitation. "I want that."

Chapter 14

Colton didn't waste a single moment.

He tilted my head back, lowering his mouth to mine in a deep, demanding kiss that brokered no room for denial. Not that I wanted to. That was the furthest thing from my mind as his tongue tangled with mine.

Backing me up, he kept going until we reached the bottom of the stairs; only then did he lift his mouth from mine. Blue eyes met mine, and my throat dried at the intensity of the passion in them. I turned and made it up three steps before his arm came around me from behind, curling around my waist. A second later, his front pressed against my back and I could feel him long and hard against my rear.

"I'm so damn impatient," he said, placing a kiss against my neck. "That bedroom seems awful far right now."

My laugh was breathy. "It's not that far."

"Fuck it ain't." The arm around my waist tightened, sealing our bodies together as he blazed a hot path of tiny kisses down my throat.

Carefully tipping my head back and to the side, I let out a soft moan as his hand drifted up my stomach and cupped my breast through the dress. With unerring expertise, his fingers found the aching tip of my breast. Then I felt his hand between my legs, and the thin, delicate material was no barrier to his seeking hand on my heat.

Without even thinking, my legs spread, giving him more access, and he took it, pushing the dress in as he cupped me. He pressed his palm in against the bundle of nerves. My hips jerked, and the sound he made in response sent a wave of little bumps over my skin. There was no control. I gripped his wrist with one hand and my other flew out, blindly seeking for the railing. I held on to both as I moved against his hand, grinding, seeking, right there, in the stairway. Pleasure built and swelled, pounding through me.

"Damn," he groaned, dropping his hand from my breast. "We aren't going to make it to the bed if we keep this up."

"You started this," I reminded him.

"True."

Pressing one last kiss to my neck, he backed off. My knees were a little wobbly as I started back up the stairs. I was already dazed and breathless and we hadn't even reached the bedroom.

The hallway upstairs was lit from the nightstand lamp I'd left on in the bedroom, and when I turned to glance back at Colton, I found myself suddenly pressed against the wall just outside my bedroom, his long and lean body against mine.

"I'm really fucking impatient," he admitted.

I looped my arms around his neck, giving in to the crazy sensations building in me. "Me too."

Colton kissed me and then pulled back. My arms fell to my sides as I dragged in air. Grabbing the collar of his shirt, he quickly pulled it up and over his head, letting it fall to the floor.

I'd seen him shirtless before, but memory didn't serve any justice. From his well-defined pecs to the way his stomach coiled tightly, he was an artwork of tone and lean muscles I wanted to touch and taste.

I reached for him, my fingers finding the button on his jeans, easily flicking them open. I caught the zipper next, and as the material folded to the sides, my fingers brushed over the long, thick length straining against his boxers.

"Fuck." His hands clasped the sides of my face again and the kiss was so much fiercer. Our teeth knocked together. My lips felt bruised, but I reveled in the raw passion.

Pressing me back against the wall, his hips pushed into mine in a slow, tantalizing roll that caused me to cry out. His hands slipped down my throat, over my arms. Pulling me away from the wall, he led me into the bedroom. Only then did he let go of my hands.

"You sure about this?" he asked.

I moved so I stood in front of my bed. "I'm sure. Are you?"

"Never been more sure about anything in my life." Toeing off his shoes, he whipped off the socks in record time. "I want you."

My stomach constricted. "I want you."

Reaching around, he pulled out his wallet. A silver foil packet appeared between his fingers. I arched a brow as he tossed it on the bed behind me. "What?" His grin turned sheepish, almost boyish. "I always like to be prepared."

"I guess it's a good thing that you are because I don't have any."

Something about what I said had an effect on him. He groaned. "Then we need to make this one count, huh?"

I watched as he walked toward me, his jeans inching down his hips. God, he was beautiful in a purely male way. I almost couldn't believe that he was real, standing before me. That we were about to do this.

"I want to see you." He slipped his fingers under the cap sleeve of my dress, drawing it down my shoulder.

As ready as I was, it occurred to me in that moment that I was going to have to get completely buck-ass naked to do this. I knew he wasn't going to want to do this with clothes on. Oh no, he was a skin man. All the confidence pranced right out of the room on two twig legs. Twig legs with perky breasts, which were two things I didn't have.

I stepped back, drawing in a deep breath as I looked up at him. I hated the sudden insecurity, absolutely loathed it. It was my skin, my body, and it was a part of me, but in this moment, it felt like an itchy, uncomfortable sweater.

Colton stepped closer, his hand lingering on my shoulder. "Are you okay?"

Biting down on my lip, I nodded as I glanced at our bare feet. Next to his, mine actually appeared somewhat small. Still not feminine. Not these cave feet. Okay. My feet didn't look like cave feet. I was being too hard on myself.

"Then what's going on? You've left this room. Probably even this house." He paused. "Is this about Nic—"

"No." My gaze flew to his, and that wasn't entirely a lie. I couldn't help compare myself to her, because hell, I was human, but it was more than that. "I...It's been so long since I've done this, Colton."

His fingers skirted down my arm. "I know."

Did he really know? "Four years."

He threaded his fingers through mine. "I figured that."

Closing my eyes, I exhaled softly. "You want to see me, but I'm not sure you really want to. I don't look like—"

"I know what you look like," he said, his voice low as his gaze met and held mine. "I have two eyes and I've been checking you out often. Enough that it would probably make you uncomfortable if you knew. I fucking adore what I see." He drew my hand to his groin, folding my palm over the rigid length. "I want what I see."

My breath caught on a soft inhale as I held him lightly in my grip. I thought I could feel him pulse. My gaze dropped to where his much larger hand folded over mine. Colton was right. He had two, completely functioning eyes. Wasn't like the clothing I wore hid what was really there, and the heat burning my palm told me that he did want this, just as badly as I did.

I could do this.

Slipping my hand away from him, I reached down, catching the skirt of my dress. I couldn't hesitate at this point. Now or never. Before I could change my mind, I pulled the dress up over my head and then I let it drop to the floor.

I lifted my gaze as I held my breath.

His eyes were glued to mine and a slight, soft smile tugged at one corner of his lips. Then his gaze dropped, gliding slowly over me, and I knew those brilliant blue eyes didn't miss a thing. Not the dainty, blue lace edging along the straps of my bra or the cups. Not the way my waist curved in and then flared out. The undies weren't sexy. They were just cotton boy shorts, and they didn't even match the bra, but as his gaze traveled down to my painted toes, I had a feeling he really didn't care about that.

"You know what, Abby?" His voice was gruff, like he'd just woken up. "You're unbelievably sexy. Every last fucking inch of you." He brushed the back of his hand over my shoulder. "This is." That hand then dropped to graze the swell of my breasts. "So are these, and so is this." He trailed a finger down my belly and around my navel. "And I want to lick these hips." His hand smoothed over one and then around, cupping my rear. "Actually, I want to taste every part of you."

My heart pounded. "I'm...I'm totally down for that."

He chuckled as he stepped closer. With one hand on my shoulder, he guided me down until I was sitting on the bed. Keeping my attention fastened on him, I scooted back and refused to allow myself to get caught up in my head again.

Not that I could when he was taking off his jeans. The way the muscles of his stomach bunched and flexed was fascinating to me. It also made me think of what he'd said he wanted to do to me, about tasting me all over. I actually wanted to do it to him.

He left the tight, black boxer briefs on as he walked around the bed, placing one knee on it as he came down beside me. There was little space between us. Neither of us spoke as our breaths danced over each other's lips.

Slowly, tentatively, Colton touched my cheek with the tips of his fingers. He seemed to map out the curve of my cheek and then my jaw, before skating those rough fingers over my parted lips. The light touch was powerfully seductive, and my response was consuming. The fire surged back to life, keeping me from getting stuck in my head.

His fingers trailed down my throat and then over each cup. My toes curled as I felt my nipples harden. He reached around, deftly unhooking my bra. The straps slipped off my arms, dropping to the bed. "These..." His voice was still hoarse. "These are perfect."

The way he touched me then made me believe that he truly meant that. He cradled the heavy globe as if it were the most treasured thing. He dragged his thumb over the rosy peak, smiling at the immediate response. He did the same to my other breast.

There wasn't a time when I knew of Colton that I hadn't fantasized about him. Only when I was married had I filed those thoughts away, but it had been so long that I dreamed of this, that I wanted this.

My mind finally joined where my heart and body already were, and when he stretched out, I did something that shocked me. Sitting up, I moved onto my knees, placing them on either side of his hips. His hands immediately settled on my hips and I lowered myself down, swallowing a moan when I felt his erection straining against his boxer briefs, hot and hard against the thin material of my panties.

"I really like where this is heading," Colton said, his hands gently squeezing my hips.

I didn't let myself think too much as I leaned down and admitted what I'd been thinking about a few seconds ago. "I've fantasized about this for so long."

Thick lashes lifted as he stilled. His stare was piercing, intent. "Are you serious?"

"So serious."

His fingers curled around the edges of my panties and then one hand trailed up the line of my back and curved around the nape of my neck. "You really shouldn't have told me that."

"Why?" I whispered, my heart thumping.

"Because I have no idea how I'm going to be able to slow this down now."

Colton dragged my mouth to his with a curl of his arm. There was nothing soft or gentle about the way he kissed me. It was fierce and passionate, a kiss of pent-up desire exploding the moment our mouths fused together, a kiss of need. He drew in my breathy moans as he circled his arm around my lower back, sealing our bodies together, chest to chest.

Everything about him swamped my senses and I whispered, "Make love to me."

Colton let out a near feral sound and then he rolled me onto my back, moving so quickly my heart nearly came out of my chest. As he stared down at me, concentration marked his features.

Then he brought his mouth to the tip of my breast. I let out a strangled cry as my back arched off the mattress. He reached between us, working the last of his clothing off as he moved to my other breast. Sensation raced up and down my body, and that was what I got lost in, the way his tongue laved at my nipple, how he nipped at my skin and soothed the sting with a kiss, a caress of his fingers.

Barely aware of him easing my panties down and then off, I was shocked and thrilled to suddenly feel the entire length of our bodies flesh to flesh. His hand slid up, his fingers splaying around my cheek, holding me there as he brought his mouth back to mine. He kissed me until there were no more thoughts, no holding back or getting lost in fear. I could feel him burning against my thigh, and my body moved on its own accord. I writhed and my hips moved, seeking him.

"You sure you're up for this?" he asked.

"Yes."

"I can't wait any longer."

I gripped his arms. "Neither can I."

He rolled, reaching for the condom. My stomach tumbled as I watched him rip open the foil and roll the condom onto his thick erection.

This was seriously going to happen.

Part of me still couldn't believe it as I dragged my gaze up to his and found him watching me. Unable to stop myself, I reached out, smoothing my hands over his hard chest and packed, tight abs. His skin was like silk stretched over marble. I dipped my hand, my fingers brushing over the sparse, short hairs. His chest rose with a deep breath and he seemed to hold it as the back of my hand brushed his cock. He made a deep sound that warmed my skin, and I reached around, folding my hand around his heavy sac.

"Fuck," he grunted. "Abby…"

Slowly, I pulled my hand back. For a moment, neither of us moved, and then he prowled over me, his strong body caging me in. Colton laid claim to my mouth, but those kisses slowed and became something…infinitely more as I felt his tip press against me. Moaning, I rolled my hips, bringing him closer, but not enough, nowhere near enough.

Colton rested his weight on one elbow as he lifted his body slightly and reached between us, wrapping his hand around his dick. His eyes, a heated and vibrant cobalt, met mine. "I want this to be good for you."

My lips parted on a soft exhale.

"No," he corrected softly. "I want this to be perfect for you. It's gonna kill me trying to take this slow."

I dragged my hand down his back as my heart pounded. "Don't take this slow. I'm ready." The peaks of my ears burned. "I'm wet…for you."

He said something I couldn't quite understand under his breath and then his hips thrust, plunging into me with one deep stroke I felt to the tips of my toes. I cried out, tossing my head back as he stretched and filled me. Nothing ever in my life had felt like this.

"Are you okay?" he asked, his voice harsh as he stilled, seated deep.

"Yes." I grabbed onto his arms as I swallowed. "Yes. Don't stop."

"Stopping right now is the last thing on my mind, sweetheart." He rolled his hips back, pulling out halfway, and then he thrust forward again. "Stopping would kill me."

It would kill both of us.

But he didn't stop. Oh no, he moved and contrary to what he said, he used slow, languid strokes as his hand brushed the damp hair off my forehead. He built a fire deep within me as his breath danced over my lips, our gazes locked together. There was a connection there, flowing back and forth between us, something intense and consuming.

It was love.

I knew that, felt it in every cell of my being, and I closed my eyes, unwilling to show him the deepest part of me because it all felt too soon, and love had never been spoken between us.

Curling my arm around the one he rested his weight on, I wrapped my legs around his hips, drawing him in even further and eliciting a ragged groan from him. I rocked my hips and he tossed his head back, his arm trembling.

"Don't hold back," I ordered in the space between us. "Please."

And he didn't.

Restraint broke. Those tentative strokes turned deep and powerful. He grabbed my hand, stretching it above my head, and clamped his hand down on my wrist as he moved over me and in me, his hips plunging wildly.

Pressure built, zipping through my veins and crackling over my skin. I cried out his name over and over as the tension coiled deep in my core. It was too intense, too much and still not enough.

Shifting his weight, he caught my other hand and joined it with the one he held. In one fluid move he had me immobile under him, completely under his control, helpless to him and yet entirely safe in his arms. Something about that combination undid me.

I came apart, shattering as the sound of his name and my cries mixed with his groans. He thrust once and then twisted, hard and deep, and then his huge body spasmed over mine as he buried his face in my shoulder.

When he lifted his head and pressed a tender kiss to my lips, I wasn't sure I was still existing on Earth. I felt like I was floating to the clouds, maybe even all the way up to heaven.

"You okay?" He eased his hand away from my wrists, drawing my arms back down.

I drew in a shallow breath. "I think I might have died in a totally...good way."

Colton chuckled and then brushed his lips over my forehead. "Be right back."

An aftershock stole my breath as he eased out of me. I was nothing more than a puddle as he rolled onto his feet and disposed of the condom in the bathroom. When he returned, I hadn't moved. Every part of me was sated, but I told myself I needed to move. Put some clothes on. He'd be leaving soon, and I didn't need to be lying here with everything on display. I started to rise onto my elbows.

"Where are you going?" He climbed onto the bed, half on his side.

"I...I thought I should grab my dress."

"Why?" Shaking his head, he snaked his arm around my waist. "No. Don't answer that question."

"But—"

He tugged me down so my back was curled against his front and his arm was a heavy, pleasant weight across my waist. "I'm not going anywhere, Abby."

I squeezed my eyes shut tightly. Could he read minds?

"Do you understand?" His voice was quiet, and when I didn't answer, his arm tightened around my waist. "I'm not."

But he would, because—

I stopped myself. I shoved that ugly part of me away. In my head, I bitch slapped it. I told it to shut the fuck up, because that nasty part sure as hell hadn't been entirely helpful in the past.

"Okay," I said, placing my hand on his arm. "I...that was wonderful, you know, what we did—you did."

"Of course I was."

I laughed lightly. "Wow."

There was a pause. "It was, Abby. It was perfect." He pressed a kiss against my shoulder. "And it wasn't me. It was you. You made this perfect."

Chapter 15

Perfect was a theme I was getting used to, or at least trying to. It wasn't entirely hard. Not when Colton excelled at making me feel like I was perfect.

A month had passed since the night Charles came through that front door. He was still in the county jail and from what I'd learned, I doubted there would be a trial where I would have to testify. Charles would plead guilty to murder and attempted murder. He would go away for a long time.

Unless Isaiah got ahold of him.

But that wasn't something I was going to focus on. Every once in a while, I had…nightmares. Sometimes Colton was there to ease those troubling memories. Other nights, it was up to me to get through them, and I did.

I couldn't believe how much could change in a short time.

While Colton had a role to play when it came to the changes I was making, the feeling of self-worth and confidence had to come from within. Yeah, the external stuff helped, but using a guy's attention to build your confidence wasn't something that would last long. It would be dependent upon him, a strength that could be flimsy.

The strength needed to come from me.

And the best way I could gain back the stronger part of me was through actually experiencing life.

I wasn't working myself to the bone any longer. Meaning after I put in a normal eight-hour shift, I forced myself to stop. Who knew how much extra time existed when you weren't avoiding…well, avoiding actually *living*?

I visited the museums in the city with Jillian, something I hadn't actually done in years, and I even started going out with Roxy, Colton's younger brother's girlfriend. Through her, she introduced me to Calla, who was dating Jax, and to Katie, a very…odd stripper who apparently had gone to the same high school as Roxy and I.

For the first time in years, I had a circle of girlfriends, and I had forgotten how incredibly important that was. When Kevin had died and I'd left New York City, it was like I'd closed a door on the life that had existed with him, including all our mutual friends. It seemed a little late now, four years later, to try to rebuild those bridges, but it was something I'd thought about a lot and wanted to try.

And like Katie had said last Sunday, while the four of us had breakfast at IHOP, "What's the worst thing that could happen? They ignore you or think you're some crazy cat lady reaching out to them?"

I was also thinking about taking cooking lessons. That was something else I'd forgotten that I'd loved—baking and all things food related. Colton was a hundred percent behind the idea, mainly because I think he just wanted to eat the food.

Speaking of the devil…

Colton reached around me, his finger aiming for the homemade peanut butter icing. I smacked his hand away. "Don't even think about it."

"I just want a little taste." He looped his arms around my waist.

I grinned as I placed the plastic lid over the chocolate cake. "You're going to have to wait."

"I can wait for the cake, but…" He lowered his mouth to my neck, placing a kiss against my pulse. "But there's another taste of something I'm not sure I'm going to be able to wait for."

My stomach hollowed in response. All he had to do was make an innuendo and my blood heated. Colton was *that* good. "We're going to be late."

"It's Jax's BBQ, not a wedding reception." His hands slid across my belly and then down my hips. He kissed the space just behind my ear.

I bit down on my lip as I leaned back into him, feeling his arousal pressing against my lower back. He was insatiable.

I loved it.

"We really should try to be on time," I said as I tilted my head to the side, giving him more access.

With his hands on my hips, he turned me around in his embrace. "We can be late."

Colton kissed me as he slid his hands down, gathering up the skirt of my dress and skating his fingers on the bare skin of my thighs. When he reached my panties and effectively slid them down my legs, every nerve ending took notice. He helped me step out of them.

We were so going to be late.

Our kisses quickly turned frantic, his tongue plunging in and out of my mouth, and our hands were greedy. One of his on my breast, teasing the aching tip through the thin material, his other firmly planted on my ass. I squeezed him through his jeans, loving the way his hips moved against my palm and the deep groan he made against my lips.

He broke the kiss and turned me back around. A fine shiver curled its way down my spine as he brushed my hair aside, then he placed his hand on the center of my back, bending me over slightly.

"Hold on to the counter," he all but growled. I heard the tinny sound of his zipper.

Oh my goodness.

I did just exactly what he said and when he lifted my skirt again, I felt him against my behind, so hot and hard.

His hand slipped around and delved deep between my thighs, and his fingers immediately went to work, testing my readiness. And he didn't have to test that out. I was already ready.

With one hand on my hip, holding me in place, he entered me from behind in a long, deep thrust. I cried out, gripping the edge of the counter. "Oh God, Colton…"

"I love hearing you say my name like that." He started moving, his strokes slow and steady. My inner muscles began to clench around him. "Fuck, you feel so good."

"So do you," I breathed.

His thrusts became harder and faster, and I came within moments, screaming his name as it powered through me. He gripped my hips now with both hands and I was drawn up onto the tips of my toes. When he came, he shouted my name as his arm circled around me, sealing my body tight to his, and damn if that didn't almost make me come again.

I could barely move when Colton turned me around, holding me on weak legs. I draped my arm over his shoulder. His warm breath danced over my lips. "Now I really want some of that cake."

I laughed as I let my head drop to his shoulder. "I'm never going to look at cake the same again."

* * * *

Roxy clasped her hands together under her chin. "Oh my God, I just want to shove my face in it."

"Please don't do that," Calla said as she passed us by, her long blonde hair swinging from a ponytail.

"I have something you can shove your face in." Reece walked up behind Roxy, tugging on her purple streak.

"Please don't do that in my house," Jax replied, appearing in the backyard, a fresh case of beer in his hands.

"We're not in your house." Reece sat in the lawn chair, dragging Roxy down in his lap.

Jax flipped him off.

"Just pointing it out, buddy." Reece grinned.

My chocolate cake with peanut butter icing had gone over well, but the scent of hamburgers being grilled had my tummy all kinds of happy.

Colton draped his arm over my shoulders as he lifted the mouth of his bottle to his lips. When he lowered the bottle, he dipped his head and pressed his lips to my temple.

"You guys are so freaking adorable," Roxy said, splayed over Reece like he was her own personal chair.

"I know." Colton grinned.

I laughed as I rolled my eyes. "He's incredibly modest."

Reece snorted. "Don't I know."

Calla headed past us. "I'm going to grab the plates and stuff. Anyone need anything?"

"I'll help," I volunteered, breaking away from Colton. Or at least trying to. He was like an octopus. I only got so far before his arm dragged me back.

He smiled down at me, revealing that one dimple. "You're forgetting something."

There was no stopping the smile when I stretched up and kissed him. Someone, probably Reece, catcalled. When I settled back on my feet and turned around, Colton smacked my ass.

"So freaking adorable!" Roxy yelled this time.

Face turning about five shades of red, I hurried in to catch up with Calla. She held the door open as we headed in. "You guys are adorable," she said as she headed for where all the condiments and plates were placed on the counter.

"Thanks." My smile was probably going to split my face in two.

She grabbed a large tray. Sunlight from the window above the sink reflected off her scarred cheek. The first time I'd seen her, I couldn't help but notice the thin slice that traveled the length of her face, but now it was something I barely registered. Calla was stunning nonetheless, and it was so obvious that she and Jax were deeply in love.

My stomach tumbled in a pleasant way. Love? God, it was something I'd been thinking about a lot lately. There wasn't a part of me that doubted how much I cared about Colton. I was fully embracing my insta-love and hugging it close.

"Are you going to be here next weekend?" I asked as I gathered up the napkins and plastic spoons.

Calla was splitting her time between Shepherdstown and Plymouth Meeting until January, when she would move up here full time. "No, but Jax is coming down next weekend."

"That's good. I love how you guys do the long distance thing."

"Me too. It's working, but I can't wait until I don't have to dread him going home or me leaving." She grabbed the now loaded up tray as I reached for the million and one bottles. Who seriously needed so many versions of mustard? The doorbell rang, and Calla sighed as she started to put the tray down. "It's probably Katie."

"I'll get it," I offered since I didn't have my hands full.

"Thanks." She smiled, turning to the backdoor. "Hurry back out. Those three guys can eat about a dozen hamburgers between them."

"Wow."

Calla laughed. "Yep."

My sandals smacked off the hardwood floors as I made my way to the front of the house. Wondering what kind of outfit Katie would be wearing, I opened the door, prepared for something pink and sparkling.

The black, silk sleeved tank dress so did not belong to Katie.

Standing on the front porch was the last person I was expecting to see. It was Nicole, Colton's ex-fiancée.

Chapter 16

A feather could've knocked my ass over. I was in such shock, all I could do was stand there and stare.

Over the past month, I thought about her every so often, just like I thought about the man I'd seen murdered, the man who ended up in the river, and the one who nearly killed me. How could I not?

And now she was here.

Since I'd only seen Nicole from distances, I wasn't prepared for just how stunning she was up close. Her blonde hair was ridiculously straight and shiny, her complexion absolutely flawless and without a wrinkle in sight. Lips plump and full and nose pert, paired with high cheekbones, she was the poster child for perfection.

There was no recognition in her blue eyes. "Hi," she said, her voice soft. "Is Colton here?"

My heart pounded in my chest and I said the first, most obvious thing that popped into my head. "This isn't his house."

And I thought that was a super-valid statement.

She glanced over my shoulder. Her hands were clasped together in front of her. "I know that. I saw his truck outside."

Then she knew damn well he was here.

"Can you get him please?" she prompted, giving me a tight-lipped smile. "I really need to talk to him."

Why would she show up unannounced at a friend of Colton's house?

Who does that? I didn't think most people did. A hundred thoughts formed at once. Maybe it wasn't entirely unannounced. Maybe she and Colton had been in contact with one another and I simply didn't know. Maybe he wanted—

I pulled the brakes on that train wreck of a thought process. Colton was an honest man, and the stupid as fuck, evil voice in the back of my head wasn't going to win.

But I realized then that I had started to turn around to go retrieve Colton, and that was like a smack in the face. What in the hell was I doing? His *ex*-fiancée had come to Jax's house looking for him—for *my* boyfriend, and I was just going to walk off and get him?

Oh hell to the no.

I faced her. "Why do you want to see him?"

Nicole blinked, obviously surprised by my question. "I don't mean to be rude, but that's really none of your business."

"Actually, it is, Nicole."

Her eyes widened this time. "How do you...?"

"I know who you are." My pulse was pounding so fast I thought I might be sick. "You're Colton's ex-fiancée."

Her slim brows furrowed. "I'm sorry, but I don't know you. You're not seeing Jax or Colton's brother."

"I'm not." I paused and then I smiled. "That's because I'm seeing Colton."

Any other time I might've laughed at her reaction. Her jaw seemed to come unhinged. She gaped like a fish out of water. My lips pursed as her eyes doubled in size. Was it really that hard to believe? Geez.

"I d-didn't know," she said after she recovered. "He hasn't said anything."

My stomach joined her jaw, falling somewhere on the floor.

"I mean, I haven't really talked to him," she quickly added, lowering her gaze as she shook her head. "I've messaged him a couple of times— called him, but he hasn't answered."

Relief poured through me, and I didn't even feel terrible for that.

Nicole cleared her throat. "I...God, this is so embarrassing." She laughed, but it was hoarse and thick sounding. "I honestly wasn't planning to come here, and I know I probably look like a stalker, but my friend lives nearby, and when I drove past and saw his truck I thought I…"

I had no idea what to say. "I'm sorry?"

God, that was pretty lame.

She laughed again and the sound was worse this time. Her gaze lifted to mine. "Do you really care about him? Because I know if he's with you, he really cares about you. He doesn't date idly."

"I know," I whispered, and in that moment, I really did know. With my hand still on the door, I exhaled softly. "I've dreamed of him—of someone like him—for a long time. I'm in love with him. I don't know if he feels the same way, but I know…I know how I feel."

Nicole's eyes closed briefly. "Make sure you tell him that," she said, her eyes filling with tears. "Make sure you show him. I…I never really did, you know? I was stupid. Don't be stupid like me." She stepped back, her throat working. "Can you do me a favor?"

"Yes," I heard myself whisper. For some reason I wanted to cry.

She smiled weakly. "Please don't tell him I was here. I'm not going to try to get in touch with him again. Not when he's with someone. Okay?"

Pressing my lips together, I nodded.

"Thank you," she said, and then she turned around. I watched her leave and then closed the door.

In a daze, I gathered up the bottles and walked outside. Everyone was huddled around the table, scooping up heaps of potato salad and putting together their buns.

Colton looked up, the look in his eyes soft, and my heart squeezed. "I was starting to get worried about you."

"Yeah, who was at the door?" Jax asked.

"No one," I answered, putting the bottles on the table as I took a deep breath. "I mean, it was someone trying to sell candles. It took me a while to close the door."

Roxy snatched up the ketchup bottle. "If it had been Girl Scout cookies, I hope you would've let them in."

I smiled as I moved over to where Colton stood, Nicole's words echoing in my head as I wrapped my arms around his waist. "If it was them, I would've rolled out the damn red carpet."

* * * *

Later that night, I laid in Colton's bed, the fine sheen of sweat cooling on our bodies as our hearts slowed. It had taken some major effort on Colton's part to pull the sheet up to our waists.

He lay on his back and I was on my side beside him. His hand trailed up and down my spine, an idle and tender caress I wasn't even sure he was aware of.

In the silence of his dark bedroom, the conversation I had with Nicole replayed in my head. It had several times while at the cookout. I hated not telling Colton about her, but I also couldn't find it in myself to break the promise I made to her.

I didn't think Nicole was going to be a problem. If anything, her unexpected visit had been eye opening. I needed to tell Colton how I felt. It could be risky. Hell, it could scare him off, but the words were burning the tip of my tongue and twisting up my heart.

And I wasn't a coward.

Worst-case scenario, it was too soon and Colton ran for the hills, but if he didn't feel the same way now, would it really change later? It wasn't like people couldn't grow to love one another, but I was a firm believer that you knew pretty quickly if love was in the cards.

I drew in a deep breath. "Colton?"

"Hmm?" he murmured.

"You're still awake, right?"

His chuckle rumbled through me. "Yes."

"Good. I need to tell you something."

Colton's hand stilled along the center of my back. "You have my attention."

I closed the hand that rested on his chest because it was starting to shake. "I...I really loved Kevin. He was more than my husband. He was my closest friend too, and when he died, I wasn't sure if I'd ever feel that way about someone else. I wanted to, but I...I just wasn't sure."

He didn't move. There was a good chance he wasn't breathing.

"Even though I was with Kevin in high school, I still noticed you and I still...God forgive me, had a crush on you." I squeezed my eyes shut. "And well, what I'm trying to tell you is that I...I love you."

He still didn't move. Or breathe.

My eyes opened and I added in a rush, "And I know it's soon and it's probably too soon for me to be saying that to you, but I wanted you to know that I do. I do love you, and I know you probably are seconds from freaking and—"

"I am freaking out."

Oh dear.

Colton rolled onto his side and suddenly we were eye to eye. "I'm freaking out in a good way."

"Oh," I whispered.

His hand curled around my cheek. "It's not too soon. Or if it is, we're both feeling it too soon."

My breath caught. "You...you love me?"

"Yeah. Yeah, I do." His lips brushed over mine. "I think I fell in love with you the moment you said you thoroughly enjoyed crepes."

I laughed as tears, the good kind, filled my eyes. "Really? It was the crepes that made you fall in love with me?"

"They had something to do with it." He kissed me softly. "And so did your sweet ass," he added, and then I laughed again. "Your smile had a lot to do with it. So did your strength. And your kindness. Everything about you actually."

"Wow," I whispered, resting my forehead against his. "That's all very sweet."

"It's the truth." His hand slid into my hair, holding it back from my face. "I love you, Abby."

With my heart full of love and my mind empty of all fears and concerns, I threw the sheet back, pushed him over, and climbed onto him, straddling his hips.

Colton grinned widely. "I like where this is heading."

Laughing, I placed my hands on his chest. "You know what?"

"What?" His fingers skimmed my sides.

I leaned down and kissed him. There was barely a space between our lips when I spoke. "I've dreamed of you for so long."

Colton picked up my hand and brought it to his mouth, kissing my palm. "You don't have to dream anymore."

My lips curved into a smile.

He was right. I didn't have to dream anymore.

Sign up for the 1001 Dark Nights Newsletter
and be entered to win a Tiffany Key necklace.

There's a contest every month!

Go to www.1001DarkNights.com to subscribe.

As a bonus, all newsletter subscribers will receive a free
1001 Dark Nights story

The First Night
by Lexi Blake & M.J. Rose

Turn the page for a full list of the
1001 Dark Nights fabulous novellas...

1001 DARK NIGHTS

WICKED WOLF by Carrie Ann Ryan
A Redwood Pack Novella

WHEN IRISH EYES ARE HAUNTING by Heather Graham
A Krewe of Hunters Novella

EASY WITH YOU by Kristen Proby
A With Me In Seattle Novella

MASTER OF FREEDOM by Cherise Sinclair
A Mountain Masters Novella

CARESS OF PLEASURE by Julie Kenner
A Dark Pleasures Novella

ADORED by Lexi Blake
A Masters and Mercenaries Novella

HADES by Larissa Ione
A Demonica Novella

RAVAGED by Elisabeth Naughton
An Eternal Guardians Novella

DREAM OF YOU by Jennifer L. Armentrout
A Wait For You Novella

STRIPPED DOWN by Lorelei James
A Blacktop Cowboys ® Novella

RAGE/KILLIAN by Alexandra Ivy/Laura Wright
Bayou Heat Novellas

DRAGON KING by Donna Grant
A Dark Kings Novella

PURE WICKED by Shayla Black
A Wicked Lovers Novella

HARD AS STEEL by Laura Kaye
A Hard Ink/Raven Riders Crossover

STROKE OF MIDNIGHT by Lara Adrian
A Midnight Breed Novella

ALL HALLOWS EVE by Heather Graham
A Krewe of Hunters Novella

KISS THE FLAME by Christopher Rice
A Desire Exchange Novella

DARING HER LOVE by Melissa Foster
A Bradens Novella

TEASED by Rebecca Zanetti
A Dark Protectors Novella

THE PROMISE OF SURRENDER by Liliana Hart
A MacKenzie Family Novella

FOREVER WICKED by Shayla Black
A Wicked Lovers Novella

CRIMSON TWILIGHT by Heather Graham
A Krewe of Hunters Novella

CAPTURED IN SURRENDER by Liliana Hart
A MacKenzie Family Novella

SILENT BITE: A SCANGUARDS WEDDING by Tina Folsom
A Scanguards Vampire Novella

DUNGEON GAMES by Lexi Blake
A Masters and Mercenaries Novella

AZAGOTH by Larissa Ione
A Demonica Novella

NEED YOU NOW by Lisa Renee Jones
A Shattered Promises Series Prelude

SHOW ME, BABY by Cherise Sinclair
A Masters of the Shadowlands Novella

ROPED IN by Lorelei James
A Blacktop Cowboys ® Novella

TEMPTED BY MIDNIGHT by Lara Adrian
A Midnight Breed Novella

THE FLAME by Christopher Rice
A Desire Exchange Novella

CARESS OF DARKNESS by Julie Kenner
A Dark Pleasures Novella

Also from Evil Eye Concepts:

TAME ME by J. Kenner
A Stark International Novella

THE SURRENDER GATE By Christopher Rice
A Desire Exchange Novel

SERVICING THE TARGET By Cherise Sinclair
A Masters of the Shadowlands Novel

Bundles:
BUNDLE ONE
Includes Forever Wicked by Shayla Black
Crimson Twilight by Heather Graham
Captured in Surrender by Liliana Hart
Silent Bite by Tina Folsom

BUNDLE TWO
Includes Dungeon Games by Lexi Blake
Azagoth by Larissa Ione
Need You Now by Lisa Renee Jones
Show My, Baby by Cherise Sinclair

About Jennifer L. Armentrout

1 New York Times and International Bestselling author Jennifer lives in Martinsburg, West Virginia. All the rumors you've heard about her state aren't true. When she's not hard at work writing. she spends her time reading, watching really bad zombie movies, pretending to write, and hanging out with her husband and her Jack Russell Loki.

Her dreams of becoming an author started in algebra class, where she spent most of her time writing short stories....which explains her dismal grades in math. Jennifer writes young adult paranormal, science fiction, fantasy, and contemporary romance. She is published with Spencer Hill Press, Entangled Teen and Brazen, Disney/Hyperion and Harlequin Teen. Her book Obsidian has been optioned for a major motion picture and her Covenant Series has been optioned for TV. Her young adult romantic suspense novel DON'T LOOK BACK was a 2014 nominated Best in Young Adult Fiction by YALSA.

She also writes Adult and New Adult contemporary and paranormal romance under the name J. Lynn. She is published by Entangled Brazen and HarperCollins.

Forever With You
By Jennifer L. Armentrout
Coming September 29, 2015

In the irresistibly sexy series from #1 *New York Times* bestselling author Jennifer L. Armentrout, two free spirits find their lives changed by a one-night stand...

Some things you just believe in, even if you've never experienced them. For Stephanie, that list includes love. It's out there. Somewhere. Eventually. Meanwhile she's got her job at the mixed martial arts training center and hot flings with gorgeous, temporary guys like Nick. Then a secret brings them closer, opening Steph's eyes to a future she never knew she wanted—until tragedy rips it away.

Nick's self-assured surface shields a past no one needs to know about. His mind-blowing connection with Steph changes all that. As fast as he's knocking down the walls that have kept him commitment-free, she's building them up again, determined to keep the hurt—and Nick—out. But he can't walk away. Not when she's the only one who's ever made him wish for forever...

* * * *

"Nope." His hands settled on my hips and my eyes flew to his. He held my stare. "And neither are you. You're done with these questions, too."

"I am?" My breath caught as his grip on my hips tightened.

"Yeah, you are." He lowered his head so that his mouth was near my ear "Want to know how I know that? You started to get hot from the moment I said fucking was my hobby." He lifted one hand and without breaking eye contact, he brushed his thumb over the tip of my breast, unerringly finding and grazing my nipple. "And these have been getting harder by the second."

Oh, sweet Jesus. The bolt of pleasure shot out from my breast and scattered, lighting up every nerve. I was struck speechless, which was a new thing for me.

"And I just want to thank you for wearing this top." Both hands were at my hips again. "I like it almost as much as I liked those shorts."

I placed my hands on his chest and slid them down the length of his stomach, the tips of my fingers following the hard planes of his abs. "Then I think you might like what I have on under these jeans."

A deep sound rumbled out from him as his hands slipped around to my lower back and then down, cupping my ass. "I cannot wait to find out."

"Then don't." I tugged on his shirt, and his answering chuckle was rough. Glancing up, I let go of his shirt. "This is only about tonight."

"Then we're on the same page, aren't we?" He stepped back and reached around to his back pocket. He pulled out his wallet, flipping it open. Out came a silver foil, and I had to laugh.

"A condom in a wallet?" I said. "So damn cliché."

"And so damn prepared," he replied with a wink. He tossed his wallet and the condom on the counter. Grabbing the hem of his shirt, he tugged it up and off. Muscles along his shoulders and upper arms flexed and rolled as he threw the shirt to where he laid his jacket.

Good God, all I could do was stare. Boy took care of himself. His chest was well defined and his waist was trim. His stomach was a work of art. His abs were tightly rolled but not overdone. He reminded me of a runner or swimmer, and I wanted to touch him.

"Your turn."

My breath shuttled out of me. I wasn't necessarily a self-conscious person, but my fingers trembled nonetheless as I wrapped them around the hem of the cami I wore. In a weird way I didn't understand, the fact we really didn't know each other made it easy to take the top off. Maybe it was because there were absolutely no expectations between us or because this was only about tonight.

Nick's gaze slowly left mine, and I stopped thinking in general. The taut set to his lips and jaw was like stepping too close to an open flame, but the heat and intensity in his gaze was what started the fire. The look was hungry, and it was a punch to the chest, stealing the air right out of my lungs.

Silently, he lifted one hand and cupped my breast. The gasp that came out of me sounded strangled. He ran his thumb over the hardened tip and then he caught it between his fingers. My back arched and a smug half smile graced his lips.

"You're beautiful," he said, voice gruff. "I bet the rest is just as fucking stunning."

On behalf of 1001 Dark Nights,
Liz Berry and M.J. Rose would like to thank ~

Steve Berry
Doug Scofield
Kim Guidroz
Jillian Stein
InkSlinger PR
Dan Slater
Asha Hossain
Chris Graham
Pamela Jamison
Jessica Johns
Dylan Stockton
Richard Blake
BookTrib After Dark
and Simon Lipskar